How Mike Met Clare

Forced to buy a suit for his parents' anniversary party, Mike first encounters salesclerk Clare in the men's dressing room...where she takes his measurements.

(*"Why can't Mikey just find a nice girl?"*
—Pris, Mike's older sister.)

When he gets the suit home, Mike discovers a very interesting note from Clare hidden in the jacket pocket. The woman who had her hands all over his body wants him to call her for a date!

(*"So I fiddled a bit with the note. I only did it so Clare could finally get over her jerk of an ex-fiancé and meet a decent guy."*
—Lucy, Clare's so-called friend.)

Though they obviously have nothing in common, Mike is willing to give his "relationship" with Clare a chance—and that's when the real fun begins....

(*"Okay, maybe I didn't give Mike such good advice on how to impress Clare. Is it my fault the plan backfired?"*
—Sam, Mike's employee and still extremely single friend.)

Dear Reader,

Imagine: You're a single woman who works in the Men's Suits department of a store. You sell suit after suit to hunk after hunk. They ask how they look, they ask about alterations—but they never ask you out. So, you slip a little note about yourself in the pocket of your favorite suit—then wait for the man of your dreams to buy it.

He buys the suit. He finds the note. But it's not the note you wrote! And that's how Clare Banning of Carolyn Zane's *Single in Seattle* eventually finds herself measuring that very man for a tuxedo....

In Carla Neggers's *The Groom Who (Almost) Got Away*, Calley Hastings practically had Max Slade all measured for a tux, too. But then he just up and left her without a word. Now, she finally finds out why when his three little orphaned brothers hoodwink her into coming to their Wyoming ranch....

Next month, you'll find two new Yours Truly novels by Lass Small and Celeste Hamilton—with a new (but probably very familiar!) name at the bottom of the Dear Reader letter. I'm taking over the reins of Silhouette Romance, and Leslie Wainger, senior editor of Intimate Moments, will now also be bringing you two terrific Yours Truly titles every month. I hope you've enjoyed the books so far—and hope you'll enjoy all the wonderful ones to come.

Yours truly,

Melissa Senate
Senior Editor

Please address questions and book requests to:
Silhouette Reader Service
U.S.: 3010 Walden Ave., P.O. Box 1325, Buffalo, NY 14269
Canadian: P.O. Box 609, Fort Erie, Ont. L2A 5X3

CAROLYN ZANE

Single In Seattle

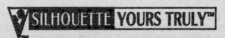

Published by Silhouette Books
America's Publisher of Contemporary Romance

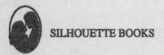 SILHOUETTE BOOKS

ISBN 0-373-52021-2

SINGLE IN SEATTLE

About the author

CAROLYN ZANE is the author of six Silhouette Romance novels and is making her Yours Truly debut with *Single In Seattle*. What's a typical day like for this busy writer?

"I'm in my partially redone office trying to get some work done when I hear my two-year-old daughter crying—or yelling—downstairs with her father, I can't be sure which. I run down to check on her, only to find that she's bored. So, my husband hands her a hammer, a real one. I say, 'Don't give her that. That's not an appropriate toy for a baby.' To which he replies, 'Hey, she loves it. I have it under control here, so go on back to work.' I'm surprised to see that indeed my daughter seems to love her new toy. I watch as she test tastes the handle of the hammer (it meets with her approval), while my husband goes back to his noisy task of cutting molding for the wainscoting in our bathroom—we've been remodeling our farmhouse for several years now. On my way back to my office, I listen as my husband shouts at the dog to leave the baby's hammer alone.

"Back at my computer I keep half an ear on the baby, half an ear on the husband, half an ear on the dog. Ah, the life of a homeowner/remodeler/wife/ mommy/dog owner/writer. It's a wonder that I'm able to get anything done at all. Especially now, when it's suddenly too quiet in the house."

Be sure to look for Carolyn's next Yours Truly, available this October, as part of Silhouette's cross-line continuity miniseries, DADDY KNOWS LAST.

To the Lord, for giving us so many reasons to smile.
And, to my dear friend Clarejoy, for being there
throughout the years.

Thanks to:
My *favorite* aunt and uncle, Joyce and Lee, for the idea.
(Still angling for that elusive title of favorite niece.)

Prologue

————◆————

"Will you guys knock it off and get over here before you get us all fired?" Clare Banning rolled her eyes expressively as her two co-workers cavorted like naughty children under the covers of the bed display over in the linen department at Monaco's Department Store. While it was true that things were slow that morning in the men's department, where she worked with these two practical jokers, they weren't *that* slow.

Clare blew her wispy bangs out of her eyes with a puff of exasperation. Was she the only person on the planet with any sense of responsibility? She was beginning to wonder.

She'd only been working at Monaco's downtown-Seattle store for a month now, but already she had more work ethic in her little finger than Lucy and Henri had in their entire bodies combined. They'd both worked here much longer than she had. Long enough to know that there were plenty of things they could be doing when it was slow like this. A shipment of men's suits had arrived that morning and needed to be inventoried, tagged and arranged on the racks out front. Lucy should be helping her with that. And Henri was already up to his Parisian eyeballs in suits that needed altering. If they didn't get started soon, they would all be out on their collective ears.

"Lucy!" she hissed, trying not to call any more attention to their area than necessary. "I mean it. You guys are going to get us in trouble."

A series of loud snores and muffled giggles reached her ears. It was useless. When Lucy and Henri got it in their heads that it was playtime, there was no stopping them. Throwing up her hands in futility, Clare decided it would be in her best interest to ignore their childish pranks and begin sorting through a sale table of men's wear.

Eyes sparkling, cheeks flushed and hair full of static electricity, Lucy and Henri flung back the colorful designer comforter and sat perfectly still, pretending to be mannequins as a customer moved through the linen section. It was a routine they had practiced to perfection. A routine that normally would have brought an indulgent smile to Clare's lips if she hadn't been in such a lousy mood.

After the customer moved on, Henri beckoned to Clare with a wave of his arm and batted his soulful brown eyes at her. "Come, *ma chérie*. Join us for a ménage, no?" he teased, his lanky young body tangled playfully with Lucy's short, pudgy one.

"No, thanks," Clare primly declined his offer and began to sort and fold a pile of expensive silk ties.

Henri shrugged at Lucy. "She is—how do you say?— party poop today, no?"

Lucy frowned as she punched Henri on the arm and climbed out of the display bed. "Shh," she chided in a hushed tone. "Don't call her that. You know how sensitive she's been the last two weeks, ever since..." Lucy inclined her head meaningfully in Clare's direction.

Disentangling himself from the comforter, Henri followed Lucy back to the men's department. "Ahh. *Oui*," he said solemnly. "Ever since Beau has gone."

Wrinkling her brow in annoyance, Clare scowled at them. "I wish you guys would stop talking about me as if I'm not here," she said crankily. She was beginning to regret that she'd ever been stupid enough to confide in these two happy-go-lucky goofballs. But she'd been embarrassed and hurt by the situation. So she'd told them everything. "And quit treating me like some kind of invalid," she ordered. "I'm fine." She smiled brightly to prove how fine she really was. She hadn't been the first woman to be dumped by her fiancé, and she wouldn't be the last.

Just because Beau was suffering from some kind of delayed Peter Pan syndrome, and had decided that she wasn't exciting enough for his new thrill-seeking life-style, didn't mean that she didn't know how to have fun. Quite the contrary. She could have just as much fun as the next woman. And somehow she would prove it. Even if it killed her.

Just not today. No, today she was more in the mood to pout. Absently she finished tidying the sale table and hoped her ex-fiancé—Beau the policeman—choked on a doughnut. The image brought a smile to her lips.

"Come on, you two." Clare grinned good-naturedly over her shoulder at Lucy and Henri as she led them to the storeroom. "Let's get started unpacking these suits."

"She is bossy for a new girl, no?" Henri teased, setting his long legs in motion and loping happily after her.

The storeroom was crammed from floor to ceiling with inventory. Muscling a large carton off the top of the pile, Henri wrestled it to the middle of the floor and cut it open for the women. Then he grabbed his tape measure and settled himself in the corner to cuff some trousers and eavesdrop on their conversation.

"You seem a little down today, Clare. You know," Lucy hinted as she slipped a pair of slacks onto a wooden hanger, "you can talk about it if you want to." She darted a glance at Henri, who looked at Clare with interest.

Clare shrugged and pulled a jacket out of the box and handed it to Lucy. "I'll be okay. It's just that..." she sighed. What the heck. She may as well confess. They already knew everything anyway, "Eva—that's my mom—called this morning. She thought Beau was the perfect guy for me. And now—" she tossed a jacket with a loose button to Henri "—she's afraid I'll never get married. Maybe she's right," she mused despondently as Lucy and Henri exchanged worried glances. "Maybe Beau was right. Maybe you're all right and—" she smiled wanly at them "—I am a party pooper."

"No." Lucy moved over and nudged Henri with the hanger, and he shook his head, more to avoid Lucy's wrath than to state an opinion. "We were just kidding, right, Henri?"

"Oui." Henri nodded affably.

"Forget Beau. There are plenty of fish in the sea. You just need to loosen up a little. Have a little fun," Lucy advised.

Clare sighed, her mood lightening with her confession. "Okay. But I, for one, am staying out of the bed display. I'd like to keep my job for at least another month."

Lucy and Henri laughed, and they worked in companionable silence for a while.

They were right, Clare thought, shaking off the funk that had tainted her morning. There were plenty of fish in the sea. In fact, there was a fish for every one of the beautiful garments they were unpacking.

"I love this suit," Clare murmured, and ran her hands appreciatively over the lovely double-breasted, charcoal gray wool jacket she held. Eventually, she mused, the right fish for her might just swim into the men's department at Monaco's and she'd be there, net in hand.... She grimaced at her ludicrous train of thought.

Then again—she suddenly felt a little reckless as an idea began to form in her mind—maybe a little fishing was just what she needed. "You know," she mused aloud, "the guy who buys this suit will definitely have a lot of class."

Lucy studied the gray wool and nodded in agreement. "And great taste."

As though watching a tennis match, Henri's head swung with interest from Clare to Lucy and back to Clare again.

As she held the suit up, a smile played at Clare's lips when she inspected its lines. "And—" she felt the laughter bubble up into her throat "—broad shoulders and muscles and—" she held the coordinating pants out in front of her "—cute buns."

"Definitely a terrific tush." Lucy nodded.

"Probably a successful businessman."

"A mogul," Lucy said solemnly, getting into the fantasy.

Henri shook his head. "All this from a suit?"

Clare suddenly grinned at Lucy and made a decision. She could be just as wild and live on the edge as well as the next woman. "You know what I should do?"

"What?" Lucy and Henri asked, leaning toward her.

"I should put a little note in the pocket. You know, telling a little bit about myself. And if the buyer of this fabulous garment is interested, I'll buy him a cup of coffee or something. Who knows where it might lead?"

"And I thought I was crazy," Lucy snorted.

"What? C'mon. It's a good idea." Clare glanced back and forth between her two dubious co-workers. Why were they suddenly so cautious? What had happened to the devil-may-care attitudes they'd just exhibited in the linen section's bed display?

"*Oui.* If you want to get killed." Henri tsked as he drew his brows together to form a straight line across his handsome face.

Clare pushed her lower lip out in consternation. "Henri, I thought you of all people would love this idea."

"I am playboy, *oui.* Stupid, no."

Lucy lifted the suit from Clare's arms. "I don't know, Henri, maybe it has possibilities," she admitted, and pulling up a box, sat down next to him.

A whisper of excitement traveled down Clare's spine, and gooseflesh began to rise on her arms. This was crazy. *So what?* she chided the overly sensible side of her nature. She could use a little danger in her lackluster life. Striding to the sloppy storeroom desk, she grabbed a claim-check pad and a pencil. "What should I write?" she asked, settling on the floor between Lucy and Henri.

"Tell him of your measurements," Henri advised, his eyes roving speculatively over Clare's leggy, athletic body. "This will bring him running, no? And we must not forget the long, wavy blond tresses, the deep blue eyes, ruby red lips and..." Henri cleared his throat and shook his head, as if to clear it of a lascivious fantasy. "Forgive me. I get carried away."

"Thanks, Henri." Clare blushed girlishly at Henri's obvious appreciation. "But I just want to have a cup of coffee with the guy, not bear his children. I don't want to give him the wrong impression."

"Oh, no." Lucy's voice dripped with sarcasm. "We wouldn't want him to think you'd lost your mind."

"Shut up," Clare groused, and touched the pencil lead to her tongue. "Let's see..." She read aloud as she scribbled on the pad.

To whom it may concern.

"That's innocent enough," she decided.

Hello. I just wanted to compliment you on your taste in clothes. We obviously have that in common.

"Hmm." She pursed her lips in concentration.

If you are single and you enjoy...

She looked up at Lucy. "I don't want another wild man like Beau," she said defensively.

"Whatever blows your hair back." Lucy looked at Henri and rolled her eyes.

... and you enjoy classical music, picnics in the country, curling up with a good book, walks on the beach and quiet evenings in front of the fire, maybe we could meet for a cup of coffee. If this sounds interesting to you, come to the men's clothing department at Monaco's, between 9:00 a.m and 5:00 p.m. Monday through Friday, and ask for Clare.

"Sounds kind of tacky, huh?" Clare laughed self-consciously. Suddenly the whole idea seemed ridiculous. What on earth was she thinking? She wasn't this hard up.

"I don't know." Henri shrugged and grinned. "I'm beginning to like it."

"Well, I don't want to get fired," she decided, coming back to her practical senses, "so let's forget it and get back to work. I think I hear someone out front." Grasping Henri's hand, she got herself to her feet, tossed the claim-check pad on the desk and rushed out of the storeroom to greet her customer.

Lucy arched an eyebrow at Henri as she retrieved the claim-check pad with Clare's note. "Oh, no—" she returned his mischievous grin "—we can't just forget this. This is far too good to just forget."

"*Oui...*" Henri's lips twitched.

"But," Lucy continued as she picked up the pencil and began to erase some of Clare's words, "it needs a little fine-tuning...."

"Modifications," Henri agreed.

"Classical music. Gag me. Now, this ought to light a fire under her little homebody." Laughing like a couple of truant school kids, Lucy and Henri made some hasty changes in the note, then tucked it into the inside pocket of the stylish double-breasted charcoal gray wool suit.

1

Mike Jacoby folded his arms across his chest and leaned against the foreign import suspended over the lube bay. He watched impatiently as his sister, Priscilla, wrapped up yet another one of her infamous real estate deals.

"I'm on hold," she informed him, and pressing her palm over her free ear, scowled in annoyance at the loud clanking and whirring of machinery that resonated throughout her brother's garage. "Yes, yes, I'll continue holding," she shouted into the instrument, pulling her earring off and tucking her cellular phone between her cheek and shoulder.

Uh-oh. When the earring came off, Mike knew from experience, Priss could be here all day, yacking her brains out. He glanced at his watch and frowned at her.

"Just a second, Mikey," she said airily, waving her expensively manicured finger in his direction. "I'm almost through."

"Yeah. Sure." Mike sighed.

Priscilla inspected the bottom of her fancy Italian leather pumps for grease. "You really should clean this place up," she complained loftily. "It's disgusting." She wrinkled her nose.

"That's because it's a garage, for pete's sake," he drawled, and pointed in irritation at his watch. He didn't have all day. As the owner of Seattle Import Repair, he had things to do. Paperwork to catch up on. Customers to pacify. Mechanics to hire. Jokes to tell. Lunch—for crying out loud—to eat.

"Anyway," Priscilla continued, picking up the threads of her conversation with her brother, completely oblivious to his censorious glare as she moved the phone away from her mouth, "I'm making arrangements at the Bay View Country Club for Mom's sixtieth-birthday surprise party. It's coming up next month, and I want it to be special." She dusted some imaginary lint from her silk pantsuit. "It's going to be formal," she stated, her eyes narrowing as they traveled with disdain over his faded and grease-stained coveralls. "So, if you don't already have one, you're going to need a suit."

"A suit?" he asked dully. Mike's shoulders dropped, and he ran a frustrated hand over the stubble on his jaw. Priss could be such a pain in the neck. He hate, hate, hated her swanky little soirees. Usually he could come up with some kind of excuse to avoid hobnobbing with her stuck-up crowd, but since it was for their mother, well, she had him by the throat.

Sam, Roger and Bart, three of his top mechanics, were hovering nearby under the hood of a BMW, laughing up their sleeves and enjoying the show. They loved watching the boss squirm. And nobody could make Mike squirm better than his upwardly mobile, power-hungry older sister.

"Yes, Mikey." Priscilla's voice brooked no argument. "A suit. A nice suit. I'm not going to have you show up at the country club wearing just any old rag."

Bart whispered something—most likely off-color—to Sam and Roger, and they howled with hilarity.

Priscilla scowled at them and turned her attention back to the phone. "Yes, yes, I'm here. Okay," she barked, "ask the general partner how many investors he can come up with. Yes, I'll hold."

Mike sent a baleful look in the three mechanics' direction. "Can it," he ordered. He could do without the peanut gallery, he thought disgruntledly.

Why couldn't Priss just throw a barbecue for once in her life and call it good? A few beers, a rack of ribs and some close friends. It had been a balmy spring—for Seattle anyway—and heck, if it didn't rain, they could have the party in his backyard. Mom would love it. And he wouldn't have to go through the evening being strangled by a button-down shirt and hundred-dollar tie.

"Okay, you can reach me at my mobile number," Priscilla said with businesslike finality to the person on the other end of the line. Shutting her phone off with the flick of a bloodred nail, she dropped it into her purse and turned to square off against her stubborn brother. "Don't give me any grief over this, Mikey. Just buy the suit. And," she warned, "you'd better do it soon, in case it needs altering."

More bawdy laughter came from under the hood of the car.

Mike pushed himself away from the car he'd been leaning against and looked down at his sister. Knowing it would be useless to argue with her, he decided to try charm.

"Priss, don't you think a surprise party at the country club will be a lot of work? Why don't we do something simple? Like, say—" he pretended to think "—a backyard cookout? That would be fun. Mom likes those."

Giving him a saucy little pat on the cheek, Priscilla turned and marched over to her Mercedes. "Don't whine, Mikey," she advised. "The wheels are already in motion. Besides," she said as she opened the car door and tossed her stylish handbag inside, "it will be good for you. You need to get out more often. A little culture wouldn't hurt, either." She looked meaningfully over at Sam, Bart and Roger, who leered back with wolfish grins.

Mike held the door for his sister as she slid behind the wheel. He may as well resign himself to an evening from hell. Once Priss put the wheels in motion on a project, there was no stopping her.

"Okay," he agreed reluctantly. "But this is the last time, got it? I hate these damn parties of yours. Next year it's a backyard cookout, and that's final."

Priscilla shook her head sadly. "Mikey, you are such a bore. You're only thirty years old, but you act like such a stodgy old man. No wonder you can't hang on to a girl-friend. You probably bore them all to death."

Mike snorted. Look who was calling the kettle black. Priss went through men the same way she went through shoes. "Just because I didn't want to join the peace corps with Shawna, or follow Joanne around the country while she toured with her band doesn't mean I'm boring. I just haven't found someone who... shares my interests yet." Hell, he wouldn't mind finding a woman who wanted to share the same zip code. He just wasn't keen on a life of one adventure after another. What was wrong with that, for crying in the night?

"Okay, honey." Priscilla's tone was patronizing. "You find some interests, and I'm sure the women will follow."

"Get out of here," Mike said, grinning easily at his snooty sister.

"'Bye," Priscilla chirped, and started her engine. "Don't forget about the suit now..." She frowned at a squealing noise from under the hood. "Do you hear that?"

"Fan belt." Mike nodded. "Bring her in when you get a chance, and I'll tune her up for you."

"Thanks, Mikey. You're a love."

Priscilla's purse rang, and before she'd turned out of the parking lot, she was closing yet another deal.

Mike stood uncertainly in the middle of the crowded men's department of Monaco's downtown-Seattle store. The cheerful piped-in elevator music bored a hole into his brain. Young mothers chased their children out from under the clothing racks, teenagers tromped by in carefree droves, loving couples inspected merchandise and—much to his disbelief—they all seemed to be having an excellent time. Didn't these people have anything better to do?

He didn't have the faintest idea where to begin. All the darn suits looked exactly alike to him. Glancing around, he tried to spot someone to assist him in this depressing endeavor. Priss owed him for this one, he decided grimly. She owed him big.

Over in one corner, a bemused customer worked with a lanky salesman sporting a name tag that read Henri. Henri—when he wasn't busy flirting with every woman who walked by—happily stuffed the patron into various jackets, pulling, tugging, patting and tsking the whole while. The poor red-faced client looked absolutely miserable. Mike felt for him.

Turning, he wandered through the aisles toward the fitting room. Maybe there was someone back here who could help. Someone who knew his or her stuff. Someone who paid more attention to his needs than the hem length of the female patrons. Someone who wasn't named Henri.

Mike poked his head into the men's dressing room. Ah, yes. There, in the fitting area, a particularly beautiful young woman was helping an older couple. If he had to suffer through the torture of buying a suit, he may as well enjoy it. Besides, she looked as though she knew what she was doing. He would wait for her.

* * *

Clare stared in dismay at the customer's unappealing image reflected—in mind-boggling triplicate—to her from the large three-way mirror in the men's fitting room. Her suit. What on earth had possessed her to have this man try on her suit? Harv was giving new meaning to the term *double-breasted*.

The rotund man cut a less than fetching figure as he stood inspecting his likeness. There were bulges where there had once been straight lines, zigs where there should have been zags. Thankfully he hadn't tried the pants on yet. Surely that would have been more than she could bear.

"You look great, Harv," his wife sighed, obviously frazzled by her husband's trying approach to suit shopping. "Doesn't he, Clare?"

Mike watched the scene with fascination, and had to admire this stunning saleswoman's diplomacy. He could tell that she was racking her brain, trying to come up with something complimentary. Quite a challenge, considering that old Harv looked like a Wiener schnitzel with buttons.

"Humph," Harv said.

"It is a beautiful suit," Clare hedged, and catching the twinkling eye of a handsome man in the mirror as he waited for her to finish, she smiled. He smiled back. He had a wonderful, sexy smile. Too bad she was stuck with old Harv here. "In fact," she confided to Harv's wife, "this suit is my favorite."

"Hear that, Harv?" his wife asked dully.

"Well, I hate it," Harv announced.

Mike watched as the saleswoman called Clare fought for her composure. She really was a beauty. Long, shapely legs, lots of fluffy, wavy blond hair swept up into a loose bun at her nape and a kissable lower lip that, at the moment, she was chewing pretty viciously. Her pale blue dress hugged her curves most deliciously and brought out the color of her eyes. He liked the way she handled the older couple, too. Cool as a cucumber.

She took the jacket from Harv and slipped it back onto the hanger, hanging it with the other suits that needed to be put back on the racks out front.

"Hi," came a cheerful voice from directly behind Mike. "Have you been helped yet?"

Mike turned to find a plump little brunette grinning up at him. Glancing at her name tag, he returned her grin. "No, uh, Lucy. I was just waiting for someone—" he gestured to Clare "—to give me some advice."

"Oh. Well, maybe I can help. What are you looking for?" she asked, grabbing Harv's suit along with several others and, motioning for Mike to follow, headed back out front.

"Hell if I know." Mike shrugged and looked longingly over his shoulder at the blond saleswoman as he followed Lucy out front. "My sister is throwing a surprise bash for my mother's sixtieth birthday, at the Bay View Country Club, and she tells me I'll need a suit."

"Hmm." Lucy's eyes wandered thoughtfully around the department, and then with great appreciation over his physique. "What are you, about a 42 regular?"

"I, uh..." Out of the corner of his eye, Mike noticed Clare emerging from the dressing room, old Harv and his wife hot on her heels. She looked as if she'd gone one round too many with the old duffer. Her hair was falling out of her loosely coiled bun, and hung appealingly around her face. And though she looked as though she could use about twelve solid hours of uninterrupted sleep, she was still one of the most gorgeous women he'd ever laid eyes on. He glanced at Lucy. What was the question? Something about being regular?

"You don't know. That's okay," Lucy said cheerfully, grabbing his arm and, tugging him over to the rack that had once held Harv's suit, began hanging up the garments she held in her arms. "We'll figure it out," she assured him.

Mike's expression became wistful as he gazed after Clare. He wished old Harv would decide on a suit and leave. Suddenly this suit-shopping business began to take on a whole new level of interest.

"Here." Lucy thrust a couple of selections into his arms. "Let's start with these."

"Uh, okay," Mike agreed, dragging his eyes away from the vision in blue. He grabbed Harv's reject and added it to his pile. Clare had said it was her favorite. What the heck? It was worth a try.

"Oh." Lucy eyed the double-breasted charcoal gray wool suit he held, and a funny little smile tipped the corners of her mouth. "You want to try this one?"

"I guess. Why not?" What was so amusing? he wondered.

"Terrific," she replied enthusiastically, and pushed him in the direction of the fitting room. "Right this way."

After what seemed like an endless fashion show for the terminally chipper Lucy's benefit, Mike finally tried on the gray wool. And much to Lucy's delight and Mike's relief, it fit like a double-breasted glove.

"Yes. This is the ticket for sure. Just what your sister ordered. Your mom will be so proud," she said excitedly. "With your dark hair and eyes, my, my, my..." Lucy shook her head expressively. "You'll be the handsomest man there."

Mike rolled his eyes. Although he had to admit, she had a point. He did look pretty dapper, if he did say so himself.

Henri, having taken a new customer into measurement captivity, led his victim into the fitting area and unlocked a dressing-room door. "Take your time," he instructed, nudging his prey inside. Turning, he stood to watch Lucy at work with Mike. "Ah." He grinned. "This is a nice look for you, no?" he commented to Mike, and winked meaningfully at Lucy.

What was with these two? Mike wondered self-consciously. Did he have something on his teeth?

Lucy smiled back at Henri. "I was just saying that very thing," she agreed. "You know," she confided to Mike as he buttoned the jacket and joined her in front of the three-way mirror, "you're going to need some alterations." She pointed to the back of his collar, where the fabric didn't lie quite right, and to the trousers that needed recuffing.

"I am?" Mike asked. He didn't know beans about alterations. If it didn't have a foreign engine, he was clueless.

"Luckily the woman who does the measuring for all of our alterations tailors is here today," she said.

Henri lifted a quizzical eyebrow but remained silent.

"If you like this suit, I'll go get Clare and have her chalk you." Lucy looked innocently up at him, waiting for his decision.

Mike liked the sound of that...whatever chalking was. However, if the blond beauty would be doing it, then he was sure it would be enjoyable, as well as necessary. And this suit was as good as any, as far as he was concerned. Priss was sure to like it. After all, it was the most expensive suit in the entire department. "Okay," he decided. "I'll take it."

"Great." Lucy grinned at Henri.

"*Oui*. Great," Henri agreed, and returned her grin.

"You *what?*" Clare glared at Lucy. "You know I don't know beans about measuring or chalking a suit! That's Henri's job. Make him do it," she cried as she picked a suit up off the floor and slipped it onto a wooden hanger.

"He can't, Clare. He's measuring a big spender right now and can't get away. I'm helping that young couple over in the corner." Lucy pointed and smiled brightly at the couple that had tried to flag Clare down earlier. "You have to do it," she urged, "no one else has time. Come on, this guy's in a real hurry." She looked winsomely up at Clare.

Clare groaned and counted under her breath to twenty. It was days like these that she wished she were a housewife. Working full-time was for the birds. "You know I haven't learned to do that yet." Her mouth quirked in annoyance.

"Look, if we weren't so busy, I'd ask him to wait for Henri. But Henri's guy could take all night," Lucy argued. Grabbing the flustered Clare by the wrist, she pulled her through the milling throng back toward the fitting room where Mike waited. Stuffing a tape measure, a tailor's chalk and an alterations pad into Clare's hands, she gave her a little push and said, "Henri says to just use one of these alterations tickets, go down the column and write the numbers in. Then just mark with chalk the areas on the suit that need attention. It's easy. Your man's been using dressing room number three. Good luck," she whispered.

Clare snagged Lucy by the sleeve. "Wait just a darn minute," she hissed, hoping that Mr. Number Three couldn't hear. "What if I screw it up?"

"You won't," Lucy assured her. "How hard could it be? Just make sure you're reading the right side of the tape. I gotta go." And with that, she was gone.

Clare stared at the tape she held in her hand. Which side was the right side? The white side? The green side? They looked identical to her. She was supposed to have learned to do this last week, but Henri had been too busy perfecting his mannequin act. Oh, well, maybe Lucy was right. How hard could it be? She shrugged helplessly and hoped for the best.

Entering the fitting area, she froze in the doorway, feeling as if she'd been hit by an emotional bolt of lightning. For there, leaning patiently against the three-way mirror, wearing the beautiful double-breasted charcoal gray wool suit and waiting for her, was the man with the sexy smile.

Oh, and the things he did for that suit. It was exactly how she'd fantasized the man of her dreams to look. Sexy, powerful, broad shouldered, broad chested and narrow hipped. Surely this couldn't be the same garment that had hung so unappealingly on Harv's portly frame.

"He... hello," she stammered, and immediately felt her cheeks burst into flame. How on earth was she going to measure this... this... *hunk?*

"You must be Clare," he stated easily, his velvety voice causing her insides to catch fire along with her cheeks. "Hi. I'm Mike."

He held out his hand to her in greeting, and Clare, suddenly awkward—because in one hand she held the alterations pad and in the other a tape measure and chalk—extended her right pinkie and allowed him to shake it. *Oh, my stars,* she thought as her cheeks flamed impossibly brighter, *what an idiotic thing to do.* She knew he must think she was a real nut case.

"Hi, Mike. I'm... Clare." *Darn.* He knew that.

A tiny smile played at the corner of his finely chiseled mouth, and his heavily fringed dark eyes crinkled appealingly.

"So, uh, you need to be, uh, measured, uh, for your alterations." Frantically she racked her brain, trying to remember what it was exactly that Henri did or said to get started. He always made it look so easy.

"Yeah." Mike turned away from her and pointed to the back of his shoulders. "Lucy said the collar doesn't lie flat, and the pants are too long and too big at the waist and, uh, something about moving the buttons... I don't know."

Clare stared at the imposing breadth of his shoulders and caught her breath. She'd helped a few men purchase suits during her short stint in the men's section at Monaco's, but never had she ever seen a man wear a suit so beautifully. It was as if he were born to it.

Unfortunately Lucy had been right. The collar didn't lie quite flat and needed to be lowered. The buttons could be moved, and the pants were too long. Although what on earth she was supposed to do about it was beyond her.

Deciding that procrastinating would only make things worse, Clare thought it best to just dive right in.

"I'm just going to chalk you and take a few measurements," she informed him, trying to affect a nurselike demeanor. If she was going to get through this charade, she was going to have to get hold of herself. Act professional. But heavens to mergatroid, it was hard. She gazed up into his lazily hooded eyes, and what she saw there unnerved her. Raw, powerful, male. He was far too virile and handsome for his own good. She wondered absently if he was married.

"Okay, sounds like fun." Mike's eyes twinkled with promise. "Do you want my clothes on or off?"

Clare frowned nervously. Good question. One that she guessed would depend on the activity he had in mind... On, she supposed, hating herself for the way this stranger could make her feel. Yes, on must be right. The customers always seemed to be wearing clothes when Henri measured them. Besides, there was no way she was going to measure this guy in his underwear.

"On," she said with a confidence that would make Florence Nightingale proud. Clumsily uncoiling the measuring tape, she stepped toward him. Glancing at the list on the alterations pad, she noted that she would need his chest measurement. "I, uh, just need to measure your, uh, chest here," she stammered, and slipped the tape around his waist and slid it up under his armpits. Holding her breath, she pinched the tape together at the broadest point of his chest and squinted at the number. The green side of the tape read seventeen inches. That couldn't be right, she thought, surreptitiously studying the well-muscled torso that lay beneath her fingertips. Unable to resist the impulse, she ran her hands lightly over the gently rolling plains of his imposing build. Stop it, she told herself sternly, a nurse would not be caressing her patient this way.

"Take a deep breath," she instructed. There. That sounded nurselike. Her hands trembled and she felt rather than saw his piercing blue gaze. Taking a steadying breath of her own, she focused on the white side of the tape. It read forty-two inches. That was more like it.

His breath fanned her neck as he watched her work, and his powerful chest expanded and contracted calmly beneath her shaky hands. Glancing up, her eyes collided with his, and her knees suddenly felt as though they were about to give out.

His smile was the stuff dreams were made of, she thought, hoping against hope that he had no idea how he was affecting her. She felt a goofy smile steal across her face and glanced quickly away. Never before had she been so flustered with a customer. Even her first day on the job. What was wrong with her?

Marshaling her powers of concentration, she tried to pull herself together again. "Okay." She noted the chest measurement on the card. Moving around to his back, she studied the way the jacket hugged his broad shoulders. His thick, nearly black hair tickled the collar, and she had to fight the urge to find out for herself if it was as silky as it looked. Her heart hammering, she drew the tape from the collar down to the hem of the jacket and wondered what to do with the measurement she found there.

Official, she reminded herself. She had to look official. Tightly grasping the chalk, she drew a series of white arrows across his back, hoping to point out the collar problem to Henri. Let him figure it out, she thought disgruntledly. Served him right for not taking the time to show her how to do this as he was supposed to.

Nibbling her lower lip, she studied the list of measurements she still needed to gather. "Uh, now I need to get the inseam."

"In where?" he asked in that silky voice that was setting her on fire.

"Inseam. It's, uh, down there." Nervous, she pointed vaguely to an area below his waist.

Mike watched her fumble with her measuring tape as she knelt down behind him. She seemed decidedly uneasy. Almost as if she didn't know what she was doing. Odd, considering she did all the measuring and chalking for the alterations tailors, according to Lucy. He could feel her hand resting lightly against his bottom as she stretched the tape down to the floor. Peering over his shoulder, he enjoyed the view as she chased her chalk around the carpet and at the same time tried to note the number on the card. She was spectacular. Absently he wondered if she was single as he watched her draw a bunch of squiggly lines around the cuffs.

Righting herself, she rocked back on her heels and looked up at him, her lovely face flushed with exertion. "You say it's too big in the waist?"

Mike nodded and pulled the waistband away from his stomach. "Mmm-hmm. See?"

She seemed perplexed. "Uh, okay. I guess they'd need to move the zipper..." Taking a deep breath, she quickly drew a crooked circle around his fly. Mike grinned. This was fun. Maybe Priss was on to something here.

"Well," she breathed, suddenly overcome with relief that she was finished, "that oughta do it."

"Already?" Mike was strangely disappointed. This suit-buying business was far more entertaining than he'd ever dreamed. Maybe he should buy another one. But only if Clare measured him.

"Yep," she assured him, smiling brightly. Taking a step back, she turned and walked into the wall. "Oops." She giggled self-consciously and waved an airy hand in his direction. "Go ahead and change into your regular clothes, and I'll fill out a claim ticket for you so that you can pick up the suit when it's ready."

She was so darn cute, he thought, watching her scoot along the wall as she felt for the door. He had a sudden, inexplicable urge to get to know her better. Find out more about her. Prolong this suit-buying business.

"Uh, Clare?"

Poking her head back into the dressing room, she smiled at him. "Yes?"

He couldn't think straight when she smiled at him that way. "I wanted my Priss, er, uh," he stammered, grinning stupidly, "sister to, uh, thumbs me the, er, give up on this suit." He stopped and frowned.

She grinned. "I know what you mean."

He grinned back. "She's planning a party for our mom, and she's the one I'm trying to please."

And for some unknown reason, he hoped that Clare liked the way he looked, as well. Then again, he realized, she must see so many guys in suits, it probably had no effect on her. The thought disappointed him. He wished he had an ex-

cuse to ask her to join him for Priss's party. But he knew
someone as beautiful as herself was most likely taken. He
sighed heavily. "So before we alter it, I just thought I'd run
it by her. Then, you know, if we need to do some more
measuring, I could come back," he offered, hoping that it
would be necessary.

"That won't be necessary," she assured him, taking his
sigh to mean that he hoped it wouldn't be. "I'll just tuck the
measurements inside the pocket, with a few notes about the
collar for the tailor, and when you come back with the suit,
he'll know what to do."

"Good idea." His eyes dropped to her hands. No rings.
Terrific. He couldn't wait to come back with the suit. Although he'd better make sure she would be here when he
did. "When do you work?" He swallowed, suddenly nervous. "I want to make sure you're here, you know, just in
case there are any problems or anything...."

"Sure." She smiled her blindingly enchanting smile up at
him. "I'll just write the days I work and my hours on the
claim ticket for you, along with my name. That way, in case
there are any, uh—" she touched her bottom lip with the tip
of her tongue "—problems, I can, uh, solve them." Holding the claim ticket up, she backed out the door. "I'll just go
do that right now."

"Okay." He grinned, watching her go. Man. That did it.
He was definitely going to have to start beefing up his
wardrobe. Two or three more suits, and maybe he'd work
up the nerve to ask her out.

2

"The preclosing is already set for this Friday on that apartment building my people are converting to a condominium," Priscilla sighed into her cellular phone as she walked around her brother, inspecting his new suit. Placing a slender hand over the mouthpiece, she frowned and whispered, "The collar doesn't lay flat, Mikey."

Bart, Roger and Sam whistled and catcalled noisily at Mike from where they sat eating Chinese takeout at the break table in the garage.

Thumbing his nose at them, Mike tugged at the jacket and turned back to Priscilla. "It needs some alterations. I'm bringing it back to Monaco's this afternoon to be fixed, if you like it."

Priscilla nodded and took her hand away from the mouthpiece. "No. It has to be Friday. Monday will be too late. Yes. Tell them to reschedule. I don't care. Just do it," she barked, and jamming the antenna back into her phone, tossed it carelessly into her purse. "You look fine," she assured him.

"Fine?" Mike asked, mildly annoyed. "I take a day off work, spend a week's salary and you tell me I'm *fine?* Some gratitude."

"I think you look bee-you-tee-ful, Mikey baby," Roger called.

Bart blew some air kisses in his direction, and Sam pretended to swoon.

"What do you want me to say, Michael?" Priscilla asked, sending a disgusted look over at the rowdy mechanics.

"How about suave? Debonair? I'd settle for jaunty." He feigned hurt feelings.

Roger howled. "That's just what I was thinking," he cried gleefully. "Wasn't I just sayin' how *jaunty* old Mikey baby is lookin'?"

"And suave," Sam added.

"I like the way his cute little tushy looks in them fancy pants," Bart drawled.

Ignoring them, Priscilla dug around inside her purse for a compact and began to freshen her makeup. "Look, Mikey, I have to get going. But I like the suit. You look great." She tore her eyes away from her reflection just long enough to bestow a superior, older-sister smile on him. "Really." Snapping the top back on her tube of lipstick, she glanced inquisitively around the garage. "What am I going to drive while you work on my car?"

Mike straightened his tie and inclined his head over at his pickup. "You can drive my truck today. We'll have your Mercedes finished up by five."

"Your *truck?*" Priscilla gasped, her perfect complexion wrinkled with dismay. "You have to be kidding." She looked with disbelief at his mud-spattered four-wheel-drive rig.

Mike grinned at his sister's discomfiture. He wasn't about to turn Priss loose on the road with his sports car. "It's either that or my motorcycle."

"Give me the keys," she snapped.

Amid much ballyhoo from Mike's lunching employees, Priscilla climbed into the vehicle.

"Drive like a bat out of hell," Mike called, grinning.

Priscilla glowered over her shoulder at him as she put the truck in gear.

"I don't know why you put up with her," Sam snorted, and brandished his chopsticks after his boss's sister as she burned rubber turning out of the parking lot. "She needs to be taken down a peg or two, if you ask me."

Bart quirked an eyebrow at Sam. "And I suppose you're just the guy to do it?"

Sam puffed his giant chest pridefully. "Thought about it."

Rolling his eyes, Mike said, "Ah, what the heck. I needed to break down and buy a suit anyway. I have a feeling Priss hasn't thrown her last shindig. I'll probably get some use out of it again sooner or later. It's really pretty cool, don't you think?"

The three men nodded affably, picking their teeth with toothpicks and slurping their tea.

"You boneheads wouldn't believe the dish and a half that measured me for alterations," Mike confided, extolling Clare's virtues. "She makes the calendar girls you guys hang in the bathroom look like yesterday's news." He pulled a chair up to the table and, after carefully inspecting it for dirt, settled down to join them for lunch. "Get a load of this lining," he boasted, opening the jacket for their inspection. "And look at this. A secret pocket." He wiggled his eyebrows and, stuffing his hand inside to display it, felt several pieces of paper folded inside. Withdrawing them, he smoothed them open on the tabletop. "What's this?" he murmured to himself.

The three mechanics stopped burping and smacking their lips long enough to look curiously in his direction.

"What is it?" Bart asked, stabbing a piece of barbecue pork and pointing it at the papers his boss studied so intently. The look of shock that stole across Mike's face had them all leaning forward.

"I don't know...." he said, knitting his brows together quizzically. "Listen to this," he instructed, and read aloud from the second claim ticket.

To whom it may concern,
Hi, there. Love the suit! If you are single, and you like piña coladas, taking walks in the rain, have exotic taste in music, would enjoy visiting the annual Medieval Country Fair, attending Modern poetry readings and heating up a cold winter night in front of the fire with a wild party, maybe we could get together. I like an assertive man who doesn't take no for an answer and who doesn't rely on the woman to provide the entertainment. If this sounds interesting to you, come back to the men's clothing department, between 9:00 a.m and 5:00 p.m. weekdays, and ask for me.

OXOX, Clare.

Mike sat stupefied as the three stooges at his side roared with laughter.

"Aw, geez," he finally groaned, much to the delight of his friends. Obviously Clare was trying to let him know that she was available. He could appreciate that. But exotic music? Modern poetry? *Medieval fairs,* for pete's sake? He groaned again.

Mike had always considered himself a meat-and-potatoes kind of guy. He detested all this snooty crap. That's what had gotten him in so much trouble with Shawna. And Joanne. And a host of other women in his past. Why did all women have to go in for this foofy baloney? Couldn't he—just once—meet someone who liked to stay at home and take it easy?

Damn. True as it was that he hated running around hell's half acre crooking his little finger and making nice-nice with a bunch of snobs, for Clare it just might be worth it. She did things to him. He closed his eyes in remembrance. Man, oh man, he thought, gritting his teeth and trying to keep his pulse to a dull roar, the things she did to him.

He hadn't been able to get her blond, perky, leggy little self out of his mind since she measured him the day before yesterday. The fantasies had been sublime. He could only imagine what a real date would be like.

"Shut up," he yelled at the three laughing—no, make that roaring—hyenas that worked for him. Once they had finished yucking it up, they demanded more information about Clare.

"Well, she's tall. And built pretty athletically, long, sexy legs and lots of terrific blond hair," he told them, describing her disheveled bun. "She's a looker, all right."

"Is she stacked?" Sam wanted to know.

Mike shook his head. "Is that all you guys ever think about?"

"Well, is she?" Roger demanded.

"Medium." Mike grinned. There wasn't much about Clare that he hadn't noticed.

Bart guffawed and tossed several take-out containers into the garbage. "If you want my opinion, I think you should go for it."

"Yeah," Sam agreed, dragging his meaty fist over his beard in a thoughtful gesture. "Ever since Shawna joined the peace corps last fall, you haven't had much of a social calendar. Who knows," he said, belching comfortably, "you might just have a good time."

"Oh, sure. You know how much I love exotic music and Modern poetry." Mike shook his head morosely and loosened his tie. "And I'd rather go through boot camp again than go to a medieval fair. What is that all about?" he groused.

"So," Sam began, pulling his hair into a ponytail at the nape of his neck, "she may not be Mrs. Right, but she could be Ms. Right Now." Bart and Roger snickered as Sam continued, "You know, my sister's husband plays the Scottish bagpipes." He looked brightly at his boss. "That's about as exotic as you can get. They're always having little concerts around town. Maybe he could tell you where you could get some tickets to a bagpipe concert."

Mike winced. He'd sooner schedule a double root canal than go to a bagpipe concert. But... if it would win Clare's favor, maybe it was worth looking into. Exhaling noisily, he lolled his head onto his shoulder and looked balefully at Sam. Maybe Priss was right. Maybe it was time he got a little culture.

"Call him," he instructed with a wave of his hand, and watched in awe as Sam, who was anything but petite, leapt out of his chair and flew—with an agility that astounded him—to the phone.

Moments later Sam returned triumphantly. "Done," he announced. "The Sons of the Scottish Empire are putting on a recital this Friday night. My brother-in-law is getting a couple of tickets for you. I'll bring 'em in to you before the concert."

It was Wednesday. If he was lucky, Clare would be free this Friday night. When he brought the suit in to be altered later that afternoon, he would ask her out. No, he thought, scanning the note again. She liked assertive men who didn't take no for an answer.

He would tell her they were going out.

* * *

"Mom," Clare protested, looking woefully at the youthful, trendy Eva Allen. "I don't think you're supposed to bring animals into the store."

"What? And leave Puddin' in the car? I don't think so," Eva said blithely, hoisting the ugly, slobbering, pug-faced Puddin' higher in her arms. Ever since Clare had moved out of the house, Eva had doted on the bundle of nerves that was her ancient poodle-terrier-et-al. mix.

Clare shrugged in capitulation, and hoped her manager didn't happen by. "What are you doing here anyway? You can't be interested in buying a suit." Her mother had divorced for the third time several years ago.

"Hardly." Eva shook her platinum blond curls out of her eyes. Her laugh startled Puddin', and the poor thing began to hack and wheeze, appearing for all the world to be knocking at death's door. "No, we were just on our way to the chiropractor, and thought we'd stop by and see how you were doing since—" Eva's face was filled with maternal concern "—your breakup with Beau."

"Oh." Clare ducked down under the cashier's counter, hoping to avoid another confrontation with her mother on the irritating subject of Beau. Why couldn't Eva just drop it? she wondered as she began straightening a stack of plastic garment bags. If the truth were told, she was relieved that it was over between them. They'd had nothing in common, and in the end she was glad they found that out before making the huge mistake of marriage. The spark that had originally drawn them together had died long before either of them could admit it.

Standing, Clare looked at Eva and—hoping to divert her attention—asked, "What's wrong? Why are you going to the chiropractor?"

"Oh, it's not for me," Eva assured her, pulling a tissue out of her pocket and wiping Puddin's weepy eyes. "I think my little Puddin's back is out."

Covering her face with her hands to hide her disbelief, Clare murmured, "Of course."

"Clare, honey... about Beau. I don't mean to harp, but—"

"Then don't, Mom." Dropping her hands, Clare cut her off. She was beginning to realize that half the reason she'd stayed with Beau so long was to keep from disappointing her mother. Beau was Eva's kind of man, she thought. And she ought to know. Her mother had married three just like him. The last one had even been a policeman, on the force with Beau.

Eva fussed with a bow that she'd fastened into the sparse curls at the top of Puddin's head, obviously hurt by her daughter's rebuke.

Clare sighed. Honestly. No one could make her feel guilty faster than Eva. "I'm sorry, Mom. It's just that I can take care of myself. I don't need a man in my life to be happy. I just wish you could believe that."

"Well," Eva prattled baby talk to Puddin', "if Clary-wary wants to be a spinster-winster, then I guess there's nothing we can do, my little Puddin'-woodin."

Exasperated, Clare shook her head sharply. Once Eva started talking to Puddin', there was no reasoning with her. Thank heavens Henri happened by when he did.

"Clare, *ma chérie,* you have a customer asking for you," he told her, and stopped to bestow a minxish grin upon Eva. "And who is this young lady with the adorable doggy?"

Eva beamed and introduced the hideous Puddin' to Henri. Much to her mother's delight, he gallantly brushed his lips across Eva's hand and disappeared into the storeroom.

"Who's he?" Eva asked, staring after Henri with obvious adoration. "He's a doll."

Shooting a beleaguered look at her mother, Clare shook her head. "Don't get any ideas, Mom. Henri is just a friend. Listen," she said, turning Puddin' and her mistress in the direction of the door, "you two have fun at the chiropractor. I have to get going. I have a customer waiting."

"Okay, honey." Eva's voice was resigned. "Call me."

Nodding, Clare kissed her mother, careful to avoid Puddin's wet nose, and set off to find her client.

It was him. Mike Jacoby. Clare felt her heart skip a beat. And, she noticed, he looked just as handsome as she'd remembered. Handsomer, actually, dressed in aging blue jeans and a faded sweatshirt that was emblazoned with the words Seattle Import Repair. He wore casual clothes just as beautifully as he wore the double-breasted charcoal gray wool suit.

He had the suit with him, encased in its garment bag and slung casually over his shoulder. He grinned at her approach, and she experienced the same dizzying, knock-kneed feeling that had left her reeling the day before yesterday. Unable to get him out of her mind since their meeting, Clare had spent the past day and a half searching the department for his reappearance.

Something about Mike Jacoby appealed to her on a very elemental level. He exuded an easy air of confidence that was hard to mistake. Not to mention the fact that he was one of the most attractive men she'd ever laid eyes on. Much more rugged and virile even than Beau. Much to her chagrin, she realized that her mouth was hanging open. She snapped it closed and reminded herself sternly that anyone with as much sex appeal as this man had to be taken.

"Hi," she said, and was pleased to note that her voice belied none of the exhilarating thrill she felt curl down her spine at his return. "What did she think?" she asked, referring to his sister.

"She liked it." His mellow voice was intoxicating.

"Great." Once again Clare felt herself go all atwitter as he winked lazily at her. What was it about this man that had her coming completely unglued after less than a minute in his presence? she wondered. Beau had certainly never affected her this way. "Then I guess if everything is to your liking... we can go ahead with the... alterations."

Mike nodded, a slow smile stealing into the corners of his mouth, causing his cheeks to dimple in a most adorable way. "Oh, yes," he assured her, his dusky eyes probing hers with an intensity that left her breathless. "Everything is definitely to my liking. If it's okay with you, we can... begin right away."

Nodding dumbly, Clare felt a delicious heaviness settle in the pit of her stomach. She suddenly felt as though she were rapidly descending in a runaway elevator. Something about the way he was looking at her made her feel as if there was a much deeper subtext to his words. But she was in too much of a dither to figure out what he was trying to say.

"That's... wonderful," she breathed, taking a step toward him and reaching for the garment bag. Her fingers tingled where they brushed up against his as he handed her the hanger that held his suit.

He followed her to the storeroom door and stood directly behind her, his eyes taking in her every movement as she hung his suit on the alterations rack for Henri.

Clare shivered beneath his piercing gaze, and tried to remind herself that she was simply a nurse—of sorts—assisting in the surgery of his suit. She unzipped his garment bag and searched the pockets of the jacket for the note she'd written to Henri.

"Do you have the alterations ticket I filled out with you?" she asked, turning around to face him.

His dimples deepened, and his finely chiseled lips quirked to reveal his sparkly white, perfectly straight teeth. "No." He regarded her languidly from beneath his thick, impossibly long lashes. "I kept it at home." Shrugging artlessly, he added, "You know, in case I might need it."

His voice was loaded with meaning.

"Oh." *Darn.* Henri would need that ticket to do the alterations. But it was her fault for not telling him that. That's okay, she decided. The chalk marks she'd drawn would most likely suffice. Henri was nothing if not the consummate professional. At least when it came to tailoring. Pulling the suit out of its bag, she darted a glance back up at him. He was still smiling at her with those dangerous, dark bedroom eyes.

Good heavens. She was reading far too much into his simple smile. He must think she was as silly as a schoolgirl, the way she was smiling and blushing so foolishly. For pity's sake, his wife was probably at home this very minute, preparing his evening meal.

Mike draped himself casually against the storeroom door. "By the way," he said, plunging his hands through the black silky hair at the nape of his neck.

Touching her tongue to wet her suddenly dry lips, Clare asked, "Yes?"

"I guess I should tell you that I'm not married."

"Oh?" She was thrilled. Although why he felt it necessary to inform her of his marital status was beyond her. She smiled what she hoped was a natural, friendly, conversational type smile. "I'm not, either."

"I figured," he said easily, and folded his arms across his chest.

What tipped him off, she wondered? Maybe Eva was right. Maybe she was turning into a spinster. Mike must have been able to spot that a mile off.

"Anyway," Mike said, pushing himself to continue before he lost his nerve, "I have tickets to a concert this Friday night, and if you're not doing anything, I thought we could go together," he told her in his most-assertive-as-he-could-without-feeling-like-a-complete-boob kind of way. He hoped she was enjoying his aggressive style and the fact that he had taken the initiative and come up with the entertainment.

Because this really went against the grain for him. Usually he liked to discuss the options with a woman before demanding a date.

At her look of astonishment, he bravely forged ahead. "I thought we could meet here, at Monaco's. I don't think the concert is too far. We could walk," he offered, hoping that it would rain on Friday. The note claimed that she liked walking in the rain.

"Oh, I . . ." Taken completely off guard, Clare searched for the proper answer to his sudden proposal. As much as she'd love to go out with him and get to know him better, he was, after all, a complete stranger. The cautious side of her nature warned her to play it safe.

"And," he cut her off, playing his trump card and hoping to cinch the deal, "I'll buy you a piña colada."

He looked so suddenly boyish and vulnerable standing there, looking at her with hope in his eyes. Her heart melted, even though every instinct warned her to decline his offer. She wasn't the type to just throw caution to the wind and go skipping off for a date with a man she'd only just met.

On the other hand, the words *spinster-winster* echoed depressingly in her head. Maybe her mother had a point. She wasn't getting any younger. And even though twenty-eight was far from ancient, her biological clock was tick-tick-ticking away. More than anything, she'd love to settle down with some nice, easygoing man and have a few kids. In order to do that, she guessed she was going to have to accept a date once in a while. Especially now that Beau was out of the picture. And Mike certainly seemed nice and easygoing. Not to mention the fact that his children would be gorgeous, if he was any indication of the available gene pool.

She felt suddenly shy as she looked up into his soulful expression. This was ridiculous. She was a grown woman. She could do what she wanted. Too bad she couldn't stand piña coladas. But if he got a kick out of buying her one, well, what difference did it make? Piña coladas were harmless enough. It wasn't as if he was offering to buy her an engagement ring....

Mike watched as conflicting emotions flitted across her face. He knew that she wanted to go out with him. Her note had given him confidence in that fact. So why was she waffling? Perhaps she was already busy Friday night.

As if she knew what he was thinking, she said, "No, I'm not busy Friday night. I'd love to go with you."

"You *would?*" Mike crowed, suddenly euphoric, then, remembering where he was, lowered his voice. "You would. Great."

"I have to work until six-thirty—is that okay?"

"Sure. The concert doesn't start till eight. How about if I meet you here between six-thirty and seven?"

That sounded fine to her. It would give her a chance to change and freshen up before they left. "Okay," she agreed, wondering what kind of concert he would be taking her to, but figuring that it probably wasn't polite to ask in light of the fact that he already had the tickets. She wasn't a huge music fan, favoring something light and easy to the harder rock and roll that most people enjoyed today. Maybe he was taking her to the symphony. She'd like that. Classical music had always been a favorite of hers. Beau went in for loud, trendy music that continually drove her half out of her mind. It was just another—in the long list—of their many points of contention.

"What should I wear?" she asked.

Uh-oh. That was one thing that Mike had neglected to ask Sam. Oh, well. Probably no need to get too gussied up for the Sons of the Scottish Empire. "Something like what you have on will probably be just fine," he decided, taking a moment to enjoy the way her formfitting mauve pantsuit brought out the roses in her cheeks. Amazing. She seemed oblivious to the fact that she was stunningly beautiful. He liked that about her.

"All right." She searched for another question she could ask. A reason to keep him there just a little while longer, but drew a blank. So instead, she just stood there, smiling stupidly at him.

"Great." He tried to come up with a reason to hang around, to prolong this little visit, but found himself suddenly tongue-tied.

"So..." Her face was beginning to ache with the effort it took to smile so effortlessly.

"So..." Mike pushed himself away from the storeroom door. "I guess I'll see you Friday."

"Between six-thirty and seven."

"We can walk from here," he reiterated, and then, because he couldn't think of anything further to say, turned to leave.

"Sounds fine," she agreed, and calling a cheerful good-bye after his retreating form, hoped with all her heart—since they'd be walking to the concert—that it wouldn't rain.

"You're going to rub the paint right off your car there, Mike, old man," Sam observed, and ambled across the garage to where his boss was laboring over the shine on his sports car.

Mike grinned. "Too bad Clare won't see all the work I've gone to, cleaning it up. I told her we'd walk from Monaco's to the concert hall tonight. The note says she likes to walk." He glanced out the large garage door into the overcast spring sky. "Looks like it might rain. Good. She likes that, too."

"Hope she likes a lot of both." Sam scratched his beard thoughtfully. "The concert is quite a little piece from Monaco's. You're going to have to hoof it if you're going to make it on time."

Shrugging, Mike attacked the wax on his hood with a clean rag. "That's okay. It will give us time to chat and get to know each other."

Sam's chuckle resonated pleasantly in his barrel-like chest. "Oh, you'll have plenty of time for that." He grabbed a rag from the pile and began helping Mike polish his car. "So, she's a fan of the bagpipe, huh?" Sam asked conversationally.

Mike's frown was thoughtful. "You know, it never came up. I don't know if she likes it or not. The note said exotic music, so I figure we'll be fine."

Sam nodded. "Probably," he panted. Breaking into a sweat, he mopped at his brow with the rag. "My brother-in-law tells me that they will be hosting a group from Australia, playing some kind of instrument called the didgeri-doo."

"Oh. What exactly is didgeridoo music?" Mike asked, tossing his rag on the dirty pile and reaching for a fresh one. His car was his pride and joy, and he never grew tired of detailing it.

"Beats me." Sam shrugged genially. "My brother-in-law sure loves it, though. When I picked up the tickets, he just said that you two were in for a real treat."

Mike grinned happily. Great. He could hardly wait. He only hoped Clare was as excited about tonight as he was.

This would be the first time in his entire history of dating that he'd gone all out like this for a woman. He'd even pulled his sport coat out of the mothballs for this one. Hung it up in the bathroom and everything, just to air it out. Those darn things smelled to high heaven. He hadn't worn that coat since Joanne—or was it Shawna?—had dragged him to some boring fund-raiser or another.

But for Clare, he'd go the extra mile. He'd shined his cowboy boots till they fairly gleamed, and spent the better part of the afternoon in the barbershop getting a haircut. He'd even ironed his slacks.

Wouldn't Priss be shocked? She was always harping on him to clean up his act and take an interest in his appearance. To get out and get some culture. Well, tonight was the night.

"Oh, before I forget." Sam stopped polishing the car for a moment and reached into the pocket of the greasy jumpsuit Mike's mechanics all wore as a uniform. "Your tickets. My brother-in-law says to try to get there early, so that you can get a good seat. Says you'll want to sit up front if you can. I guess you can hear better up there or something."

"Didgeridoo and Bagpipes Too," Mike read, taking the tickets from Sam. Perfect.

"Thanks, buddy." Mike's eyes glowed with anticipation. "I owe you one."

"Anytime." Sam puffed, scrubbing the last traces of wax off his boss's car. "Anytime."

"Hi, Mom." Clare kicked off her shoes and settled back with the phone to enjoy her Friday-afternoon break. Lucy and Henri were out front—hopefully not in the linen department's display bed—and she had the cluttered storeroom all to herself.

"Clare?" Eva asked. "Where are you?"

"At work. I'm on my break. Just thought I'd call to find out how Puddin's doing." Actually Puddin's condition was neither here nor there, as far as she was concerned. She just felt like running her date with Mike past her mother.

"Oh, that's so sweet," Eva said. "My little Puddin's in traction. Poor thing has a slipped disk."

"That's too bad." Clare tried to sound concerned, but the image of the fat, balding Puddin' in traction blew her mind.

"Oh, I think he'll be okay. They've got him in a tiny little back brace. It's so cute. Try not to worry, honey. It's only for a few more days."

"I'll try," she assured her mother. "Listen, Mom?"

"Hmm?"

"I just wanted to let you know that I have a date tonight. I'm going to a concert."

"A date to a concert?" Eva squealed with delight. "With Beau?"

Clare sighed. Her mother had a one-track mind. "No, Mom. Beau and I broke up, remember?"

"Yes." Her mother's voice was petulant. "Who, then?" Her tone brightened. "That darling Frenchman?"

Wincing, Clare shook her head. "No, not Henri, Mom." Just the thought of dating the playful Henri was exhausting. "His name is Mike Jacoby. I met him here, at the store. He came in to buy a suit."

"Oh. How long have you known him?"

"We just met."

"And you're going out with him? Tonight?" Eva asked, surprised. "That's not like you." She chuckled. "He must be pretty special. What does he do for a living?"

Clare shook her head. Funny, she had never thought to ask. "I don't know...."

"Where does he live?"

"Uh..."

"At least tell me where this concert is," Eva demanded, growing impatient with the lack of details.

"Well..."

"Oh, Clare."

"You're right." Clare nervously twisted the phone cord around her thumb. "This is crazy. I don't even know this guy. What was I thinking? I'm going to tell him I can't go." What *had* she been thinking? She didn't know the first thing about this guy. Just because he looked nice didn't mean he was.

"Don't you dare," Eva cried. "Did I say not to go? I was just curious about him, that's all. I'm thrilled that you are going on a date. If you like him, then I'm sure he's a very nice boy. Go. Have fun," her mother instructed. "When is he picking you up?"

At least she knew that much. "In a couple of hours." She nervously chewed the phone cord. It was too late to back out anyway. She would just have to hope that her walk on the wild side didn't land her in trouble. "He's coming to the store. We're going to walk to the concert from here."

"In the dark?" Eva was incredulous. "It's cold outside."

"I guess he likes getting out in the fresh air," Clare sighed, and pounded her forehead with the palm of her hand.

Eva laughed. "I like him already."

That was not a good sign, Clare thought as she told her mother goodbye and hung up. No, the fact that Eva already liked this guy was not a good sign at all.

She laughed. "I like this already."

That was no a good sign. Marie figured she'd had too

3

"Do you think the heels are a bit much?" Clare asked Lucy as they stood in front of a dressing-room mirror later that evening. It was a quarter to seven and Mike would arrive any minute. Nervously she stared in dismay at the ridiculously high-heeled sandals that were clinging to her feet by a few thin straps of leather. What had possessed her to pick these shoes for tonight's date with Mike?

Taking a deep breath, Clare tried to quell what felt like a flock of birds flying south in her stomach. She wished she had more time. And she wished she'd brought a pair of flats. But most of all, she wished she'd told Mike that she was busy.

Lucy inspected her footwear with admiration. "I think you look fantastic. Those shoes do wonderful things for your long legs. Besides, he's really tall, so what's the problem?"

"Nothing, I guess. They just hurt my feet, that's all." It was true. She couldn't have been in any more pain if she'd strapped a couple of mousetraps on her feet. No wonder she never wore these silly shoes anywhere.

The fact of the matter was, the whole darn outfit was incredibly uncomfortable. She'd inadvertently bought a pair of petite panty hose, and much to her irritation, the waistband was heading toward the hemline of her skirt. How she was ever going to cross her legs once they were seated was a mystery to her. Probably for the best, she thought, sighing down at the snug, formfitting skirt that hugged her hips and thighs most annoyingly. The skirt wouldn't allow her to cross her legs, even if she'd wanted to.

"Maybe I should change back into the outfit I wore to work today." She looked hopefully at Lucy. "At least then I'd be comfortable."

"Will you stop?" Lucy cried, exasperated. "You look great. You want to make a good impression on him, don't you? This outfit will make him sit up and take notice for sure," she said, reaching over and fingering the sheer wisp of lacy fabric that made up the sleeve of Clare's blouse. "Beau certainly couldn't accuse you of being a party pooper in this getup."

"True," Clare murmured doubtfully. Lucy did have a point. Certainly, if she'd attempted to be a little more adventurous in the past, she and Beau would still be together, and she wouldn't have to go through the trauma of a first date with Mike. Too bad Beau hadn't been worth the effort.

Mike, on the other hand, was a different story.

She leaned toward the mirror and began to apply a coat of Passion Plum lipstick. She wasn't big on gobs of makeup, either. Why, she wondered morosely, couldn't she be more like the girls in the beer commercials? Never in her entire youth had she ever danced in her bikini at a beach party with carefree abandon, giggling and jiggling and mindlessly hanging on the arm of some muscle-bound, beer-chugging beach bum.

It just wasn't her idea of a good time. If she went to the beach at all, it was with a good book and a gallon of sunscreen. Well, she thought, perhaps it was time to try something new. To boldly go, and all that nonsense.

"Okay," Clare mumbled, blotting her lips on a tissue, "I guess I'm as ready as I'll ever be."

"Not yet," Eva sang, pulling open the door of the dressing room, Puddin' in his back brace tucked under her arm. "Hi." She smiled at Lucy. "I'm Clare's mom, you can call me Eva. This is Puddin'." She took Puddin's limp forepaw and waved it at Lucy.

"I'm Lucy." Waving back at the loudly groaning and snorting Puddin', she grinned at Clare.

"Mom! What are you doing here?" Clare demanded, her distress reaching a crisis point. She wasn't ready to introduce her mother to Mike yet, let alone the mangy Puddin'. How would she ever explain the contraption the poor thing was wearing? It looked for all the world like a bird cage.

"Now, now, calm down." Eva squeezed into the dressing room with the two young women and propped her Puddin' in the corner. Standing, she smiled brightly at her daughter. "That nice Henri told me where I could find you. I brought you a present," she announced, and rummaging around in her purse, withdrew a small package.

"Mom, couldn't this wait?" Clare groaned. Trust Eva to turn a first date into a holiday-gift exchange.

"No," Eva chirped. "Go on. Open it."

Clare quickly did as she was told. She wasn't the type to keep a man waiting, as Mike most undoubtedly was by now. Sometimes it was just easier to go with the flow where Eva was concerned. "A bra?" she asked, her eyes widening in surprise.

"Not just any bra." Eva beamed. "A forty-eight-hour SuperBra!"

Lucy eyed the bra appreciatively. "Oh, yes," she nodded. "Those are great."

"No way," Clare exclaimed, shaking her head and thrusting the bra back into Eva's hands. "I'm uncomfortable enough as it is."

Eva's face crumpled. "But..."

"Forget it, Mom."

"Honestly," Eva declared, glancing at Lucy, "how did I ever end up with such a stick-in-the-mud daughter? I'm always telling her to loosen up, but will she listen to me?"

Lucy shook her head in sympathy. "I've been trying to tell her the same thing, but she won't listen to me, either."

Clare rolled her eyes. "Oh, for the love of... Give me that," she groused, grabbing the bra.

"Clare?" Mike's sexy baritone filtered in to them from somewhere beyond the fitting room. "Are you ready?" His voice grew steadily closer.

"I'll be right there!" she called, feeling the flock in her stomach take wing. Sternly eyeing Lucy and her mother, she quickly unbuttoned her blouse and whispered, "Now you two please just stay in here and be quiet. I don't want to overwhelm the poor guy before we've even had our first date."

Eva and Lucy nodded chummily.

"Clare?" The sound of Mike's voice came from just outside the dressing-room door.

Trying not to panic, Clare held her finger to her lips and frantically began untangling the forty-eight-hour SuperBra. The straps were caught on the ribbon Eva had used to wrap her gift. "Yes?"

"Oh, there you are." There was a smile in his voice. "We should probably get going."

"Uh, sure." Fumbling around in the crowded dressing room, Clare spun around, twisting to and fro and attempting to discreetly deposit her bustline into her new SuperBra. Puddin' snorted.

"Are you okay?"

"Uh, sure." She scowled at Eva. "Just have a case of the, uh, sniffles." Puddin' hacked and wheezed.

"Oh." Mike stood uncertainly outside the dressing-room door. Sounded worse than a case of the sniffles to him. If the congestion in her cough was any indication, he should be taking her to an emergency room. "Are you sure you're okay?"

"I'll be fine. Really."

"Okay." He hoped so. It was raining lightly outside. It wouldn't do for her to get a chill. "I'll wait for you out front," he told her, spotting a chair just beyond the fitting area.

"Great," she called, and snorted again.

Taking his seat, Mike reached into his sport-coat pocket and retrieved the Didgeridoo and Bagpipes Too tickets. *Hmm,* he thought, inspecting them for the concert location, *the Armory.* Sam had assured him that they could walk to the concert from Monaco's. But according to the tickets, the Armory was down by the docks. Had to be at least twenty blocks. Maybe more.

No problem, he thought jovially, if walking was her thing, he'd grin and bear it. He wasn't about to make the same mistakes he'd made with Shawna and Joanne. Not with Clare. No, there was something really special about Clare. He smiled smugly. He was a lucky son of a gun. He could hardly wait to see her reaction when she discovered that he'd found some exotic music for her.

He shifted impatiently in his seat. What was taking so long? If they were going to stop for a drink, they would have to get a move on. He glanced at his watch.

"Hi," Clare said shyly, stepping out of the fitting area a moment later. Moving over to where he sat waiting, she paused and looked expectantly at him. "I'm ready."

Mike leapt to his feet. She was more than simply ready, he thought, taking in the vision that appeared before him. She was breathtaking. His libido raced through an assortment of mental gymnastics as he stood staring at her. Her long, slender legs seemed to go on forever under her skimpy little skirt, and her generous cleavage peeked fetchingly above the neckline of her blouse. She'd forgone her usual bun for a wild, free-flowing hairstyle that nearly had him fainting from lack of oxygen. She looked terrific. The guys at the garage would go crazy over her. Not that they would ever get the chance to meet her, he thought grimly. No, he was keeping this one all to himself.

"Great," he said when he could finally breathe. "We're right on time." He took her coat from her hands and, stepping behind her, helped her into it. "In fact, we could stop for your piña colada now, before the show, if you like." At the consternation in her expression, he changed horses. "Or if you prefer, we could wait until after...." He hoped that she wanted it now. He could use a stiff drink to get him through an evening of bagpipe and didgeridoo music.

"Uh..." Clare frowned, puzzled by his need to buy her a piña colada. What exactly was it with him and piña coladas? She took a deep breath and turned to smile at him. He was so amazingly handsome. Never mind, she decided. If he liked piña coladas so much, she would learn to like them, too. After all, she'd resolved to be more flexible about the lust-for-life mind of the American male. May as well start here.

"That would be lovely." Reaching around behind her neck, she flipped her hair out from beneath her coat collar and nodded and smiled engagingly. "A piña colada after the concert would be just fine."

The tiny lines that forked at the corners of his eyes crinkled. He took her arm and led her toward Monaco's main entrance. "Since you enjoy walking, I'll leave my car here in the lot. The concert is being held down by one of the docks near Elliot Bay," he informed her, "so we have plenty of time to enjoy the weather."

"Oh?" Clare nibbled the inside of her cheek. Where did he get the idea that she enjoyed walking? He seemed to take some things for granted. Although, she thought charitably, perhaps he figured that since she spent a lot of time on her feet here at the store, that she was an upright sort of person, so to speak. "That's . . . nice." She tried to smile past the pains that were already shooting through her toes.

Good heavens. She hadn't even gotten to the door yet, and her feet were already killing her. How on earth would she ever make it to the docks? They were at least twenty—maybe more—blocks away. And unfortunately, she noticed as she peered out through the glass entrance doors, it was beginning to rain in earnest. She glanced down at her shoes. She wouldn't think about it.

As they exited the department store, Mike noticed gratefully that it was beginning to rain in earnest. He glanced down at Clare's feet. Those shoes did awesome things for her legs. She looked sexy as all get out. And she had the cutest little toes. He'd never understand how women did it. Walked for miles in those pointy little torture devices, and made it look so easy. In the rain, even. As it was, his comfortable cowboy boots were going to give him a blister.

As they strolled quickly along, Clare was grateful at least that she had Mike's arm to cling to when it came to fording the really deep puddles and streams that seemed to be growing at an alarming rate. Although, if he had a perfectly good car sitting back in the lot, she had to wonder why they were putting themselves through this ordeal. Maybe he figured she'd be more comfortable on a first date, not locked in a car with a virtual stranger, she thought loyally. Yes, that must be it.

"This rain is certainly refreshing," Mike called as they rushed to a crosswalk, only to have the light change just as they arrived.

"Yes," Clare panted, hippity-hopping rapidly along, struggling to keep up with his long strides. "It's quite—" she searched for the proper word "—invigorating."

A city bus roared by, soaking them both to the skin.

"*Wooo!*" Clare laughed, what she hoped was a good-natured, adventurous, lust-for-life kind of laugh. "Now, that's what I call...*refreshing!*" Her heart sank with the knowledge that her mascara must be running in black rivers down her cheeks and the hairdo that she labored over was lying in limp ropes down her back.

Wow, Mike thought. She sure was a good sport. Most women would have had a heart attack over the tsunami that bus had kicked up. He glanced once more at his watch. This was taking much longer than he'd figured. If they were going to get good seats, up front as Sam had suggested, they were going to have to step it up.

Thankfully the light changed, and Mike took her arm and hustled her across the street.

He must have been a Boy Scout at one point, Clare thought, enjoying his chivalry despite the torrential downpour. Reaching up, she pushed her soggy tresses out of her eyes, and tried not to think about the pain that shot through her feet with each torturous step. The city blocks rose and fell, becoming a blur of agony, and the rain made any kind of intelligent conversation impossible. It was becoming increasingly clear that they would either have to hail a cab, or Mike was going to have to hoist her up onto his back and drag her the rest of the way. And if the pain in her feet wasn't bad enough, her skirt seemed to be shrinking. Would he think it unseemly of her to stop, rip her panty hose off and stuff them into her purse? As it was, they were riding down around her knees....

"We're nearly there," Mike shouted at her through the downpour. He seemed to be limping.

Nodding, Clare smiled up at him, and thought she'd weep with joy. He was right, she noted with relief. Elliot Bay loomed just ahead on the horizon. She racked her brain, trying to remember ever hearing of a concert hall down by the docks.

"How are you doing?" Mike stopped once they finally reached First Avenue and squinted through the deluge into her face. The wrap she was wearing seemed a little too light for this downpour. Water sluiced over her head, onto her shoulders and ran in rivulets down the front of her lithe body, molding her clothing with little subtlety to her intriguing form. He hoped she was warm enough. The way she'd been coughing back there in the dressing room, she couldn't be too careful.

"I'm fine." Her voice was a sultry contrast to the inclement weather as she blinked up at him.

Raindrops hovered like so many tiny crystals on her lashes, and her lips were sparkling and dewy. No wonder she liked walking in the rain so much, he thought, his heartbeat pulsing more loudly than the rain in his ears. She took to it like a duck to water. He fought the sudden urge to pull her into his arms and taste the drops he found at her lips.

Shaking his head to clear it, he could see water spray from his hair in all directions. He felt like a drowned rat. Next time they went out on a date—if there was a next time—he was going to drive. Of that he was certain. Because no matter how much the little mermaid at his side was enjoying their swim, he was beginning to lose the sensation in his fingers. And toes. And a few other vital organs in between.

Luckily they had finally arrived in front of the Armory building.

"I think this is the place." Mike pulled her close, drawing his mouth to her ear so that she would be able to hear him above the wind. He looked across the street at the run-down Armory, and felt the disappointment settle like a brick into the pit of his stomach. The institutional green paint was peeling and covered with graffiti, and the windows, many of which were broken or boarded-up, gave the place a look of desertion.

Could Sam have been mistaken? He stood with Clare, staring through the slanting rain at the building, the muscles of his jaw twitching in agitation. There was no way in hell he was going to walk another step. If this wasn't the place, he'd hail a cab and buy her that piña colada. The mood he was in, he could cheerfully down several himself. The heel of his left foot felt as though it had been attacked by a pack of wild jackals. He wondered absently if Clare had a Band-Aid in her purse.

"Well..." Clare tried to keep her tone light. "We may as well go inside." She wouldn't have cared if the place had been a maximum-security penitentiary. She was going to get out of this rain or know the reason why.

Mike smiled down at her, took her elbow in his hand and guided her around several potholes to the front door of the Armory. He loved the way she seemed so eager to go inside, despite the seamy appearance of the old building. What a trouper. Shawna would have shot him by now.

A small sign tacked in the porch wall read Didgeridoo And Bagpipes Too, Tonight. Downstairs In Concert Hall A. Mike's sigh of relief was audible. Thank heavens. This was indeed the place.

Much to her mortification, Clare was amazed to discover that this was the place. The stale, musty air assailed her nostrils as Mike opened the door and assisted her inside. Could he be serious? This was the activity she'd looked forward to with such excitement? Gamely she decided to give him the benefit of the doubt. He must know something she didn't know about the bagpipes. Perhaps it had been underestimated as a romantic instrument.

Their shoes clicked and clomped noisily as they walked across the squeaky old wooden floor to the staircase that led down to the basement and Concert Hall A. The sounds of what had to be bagpipes and didgeridoo's warming up echoed through the old hallways to them as they descended. Clare tried to mask her trepidation with a smile.

Pausing at the landing, both Mike and Clare privately had the absurd urge to bolt. To cut their losses before they got in too deep. But as they gazed into each other's eyes and smiled at each other through their mutually gritted teeth, they changed their minds, each deciding to enjoy this evening for the sake of the other.

"Sounds...interesting," Clare murmured, referring to the screechy toots and whistles that grew louder at their approach. Looking up into his ruggedly handsome face, she knew that watching someone stand on his head and stack marbles would most likely be interesting if Mike was there with her.

"Yes," Mike agreed. "Interesting."

As they reached the basement, Clare noticed that Mike had to duck to keep from hitting his head on the ceiling. He was so tall. At five feet, eight inches, she'd always fancied herself to be pretty tall. Especially in these heels. But he had a way of making her feel petite and feminine as he led her to the room from where the music was emanating.

Clare couldn't be certain as they entered the tiny room, but the two dozen or so fans that had assembled for this concert all appeared to be at least as old as her grandparents. A small card table was situated against the far wall and held a plate of homemade cookies and an urn of what smelled like instant coffee. All eyes turned to stare at them as they arrived.

Bravely Mike took her hand in his and pulled her to the front row. As they took their rickety, metal-folding-chair-type seats, he asked Clare if she would care for a cup of coffee.

"Yes," she breathed gratefully, removing her coat and plucking at the soggy lace of her blouse with her fingertips, trying to unobtrusively extract it from the excruciating SuperBra. "That would be marvelous." She wished he would bring her a couple of extra cups, one for each foot. Her feet felt like two bricks of ice. Blistered bricks.

Mike scooted between the bandstand—where several old codgers were warming up their instruments—and the folding chairs till he reached the refreshment table at the far wall. Clare took the opportunity to find her compact and inspect her appearance.

Unfortunately, she moaned inwardly as she stared at her reflection, there wasn't much she could do without a blow-dryer and a hot bath. Pushing her limp, bedraggled hair away from her face, she applied a little powder to her nose, dabbed at her running mascara and freshened her lipstick. It was hopeless, she sighed, and let her eyes wander around the dilapidated room till they landed on Mike.

He stood, holding two cups of coffee and a napkin that she suspected held some cookies and laughed patiently at something an old man wearing a kilt was telling him. Her stomach grumbled. In the excitement of getting ready for her date with Mike, she'd forgotten to eat lunch. She hoped Mike had snagged her several cookies.

He looked so adorable, standing there, hunched over so that he could hear what the little old Scotsman was telling him. There was something about Mike Jacoby that made a person feel comfortable, she thought. Even in the most horribly uncomfortable situation. Shifting her weight, she searched for a less painful position in her folding chair, and tried to stretch her skirt down over her knees.

"This was all I was able to get for us without seeming greedy," Mike said, arriving at her side. He grinned and handed her a cup of coffee and a cookie.

"This will be fine," she said, hungrily eyeing the cookie. She gestured to the Scotsman. "What was he saying to you?" she asked politely, trying to make conversation.

"Billy Bob? He just wondered if we were fans of the didgeridoo."

"Ah," she said noncommittally. Her shiver was involuntary as the warmth of the cup traveled up her fingers and began to thaw her hand.

Settling into his own less than sturdy chair, Mike carefully removed his waterlogged overcoat and wiggled his toes—still numb from the cold—in the snug confines of his boots.

Again his eyes traveled to Clare's dainty feet, scantily clad in her skimpy sandals. Even her feet were sexy, he thought, allowing his mind to relax. He'd never met a woman who could trudge so gamely through the elements and still look like a goddess. His blood ran hot as images of Clare, wearing nothing but a bath towel and stepping all pink and squeaky clean from a shower, tripped through his brain.

Clare frowned and glanced around the room. "Do you smell mothballs?" she asked, sniffing the dank air that slowly circulated throughout the basement.

Mike nodded and sniffed with her, searching for the origin of the powerful odor until he, much to his chagrin, realized it was coming from his damp sport coat. "This is an old building," he commented, and hoping to divert her attention, shifted slightly away from her.

"True." A bemused smile touched her lips. "Nearly as old as the audience. We're definitely the youngest people here tonight."

"So I noticed." He was going to have to remind Sam that the note had said exotic music, not prehistoric, he thought churlishly. She must think he was a real lunatic, bringing her to this place before her sixty-fifth birthday.

"So," she said, and turned toward him in her seat, unaware of the captivating picture she made as she gazed up at him through those baby blue eyes of hers, "I was just wondering if you'd mind explaining to me what didgeridoo music might be?"

Mike stared at her, suddenly at a loss for words. Hell, he didn't know. He'd never heard of a didgeridoo until Sam's brother-in-law had come up with this bright idea. For crying out loud, exotic music was her bag, wasn't it? He'd hoped to ask her the same question.

Now, ask him about the Beatles, and maybe he could hum a few bars.

Remembering Sam's words, he tried to affect a mysterious expression and said, "Wait and see. I can tell you this, though, you're in for a real treat." At least he hoped so. So far, this whole evening had been nothing to write home about. Unless, of course, he counted simply spending time with the delectable Clare Banning.

As he removed his sport coat, the stench of mothballs once again filled the air. He threw it on the floor and kicked it under his chair. When he got home, he decided with disgust, he would burn it. Laying his arm across the back of Clare's folding chair, he lightly fingered a damp tendril of her hair. Her hair was incredibly soft, he thought, stroking the blunt ends with his fingertips.

Clare leaned back in her seat and relaxed, soaking up the sensation of Mike's arm casually draped around her shoulders. There was something so innately protective in the gesture. It was almost as though nothing bad could ever happen if Mike was there to watch over her.

The elderly Scotsman, kilt flapping at his knobby knees, finally made his way up to the bandstand and adjusted the mike down to his mouth. Ignoring the horrendous feedback that screeched and whined throughout the PA system, he proceeded to welcome the sketchy crowd to the Sons of the Scottish Empire's Didgeridoo and Bagpipes Too night.

Why on earth a PA system was necessary in a room this small, Clare would forever wonder. It was hardly more than a closet.

"Tonight," the Scotsman announced in a thick Texas accent, "we have a special treat for y'all. The Sons of the Australian Empire have agreed to join the Sons of the Scottish Empire for a recital that we believe y'all won't be able to see anywhere else."

Yes, Mike thought smugly. An exclusive concert. He slid a sideways glance at Clare. She really ought to love this. His eyes moved to the subtle curve of her lips. Maybe, if she was really pleased, he'd get a good-night kiss out of the deal.

Clare could feel Mike studying her for her reaction, and did her best to look completely enraptured by the idea that she was one of the few lucky ones to witness such a momentous—and evidently historical—occasion. It was so obvious that he was trying to please her. The sweetness of his effort touched her.

The Australian aboriginal group was summarily introduced by the kilt-wearing Billy Bob, and its leader began giving some background on his music.

"Our music is of much importance to us. It is how we tell the stories to our children of our life. We use click-stick sometimes and sometimes we use boomerang. But we play the didgeridoo most of the time." He demonstrated by bringing the instrument to his lips and pointing it at the microphone, gave a blast that reminded Clare of bathwater as it noisily gurgled down the drain. *Noisily* being the operative word, she thought, wincing. Quickly peeking over her shoulder, she noticed several of the seniors turning down their hearing aids.

"We make didgeridoo from the branch of a tree, which the termite eats out to make hollow, like a tube. We cut this tube, about one yard, as you say, long, then clean it, painting the outside white, or maybe red with clay. Didgeridoo is played like trumpet, but a little different. The player doesn't stop blowing. He fills his cheeks with air, then takes a quick breath through the nose. He can do this at the same time... blow air from his cheek and breathe in and out. A good didgeridoo player...he can go on for ten minutes with the same sound, and not stop."

For the next ten minutes, what Clare could only assume was an excellent player, played. And played. And...played. She tried to tap her foot to the beat, but unfortunately there was none.

How on earth did a guy like Mike ever get into the didgeridoo? she wondered. Then again, how on earth did *anyone* get into the didgeridoo? It only made her realize that she hardly knew anything about him at all. He just didn't seem like a didgeridoo kind of fan. He seemed more like an oldies-rock kind of guy.

Booiiiing-doooooo-boing-dooooo-dooooooo.

Mike stared at his boots and fought the violent urge to laugh. The urge to laugh, and laugh hard. The kind of laughing he couldn't control. The kind of laughing that he didn't want to laugh, back in grade school, but got sent to the principal's office for anyway.

He pinched the back of his knee with the hand that wasn't resting at Clare's shoulder. He bit his tongue till it nearly bled. He tried to think of anything but the didgeridoo, and the broken-down Armory building and Billy Bob, the kilt-wearing Texan, but it was hard.

The aboriginal continued, "A very good didgeridoo player can make sounds like the laughing cuckoo bird..." Much to Mike's regret, he demonstrated. "Or make sounds like the howl of the native dog. The dingo." *Yip yip, boow-woow, boingggggg-doooooo, bow-wow.*

Mike sank his teeth into his cheek. He'd wanted so badly to impress Clare, he thought wildly. And now he was going to ruin it all by uncontrollably laughing his fool head off. He could feel the mirth beginning to rise into his throat, clawing its way past the panic that was already in residence.

Thankfully Billy Bob jumped up onto the stage, grabbed the mike and asked for a round of applause, and Mike was able to stave off the laughter for a moment. But his good fortune did not last. Oh, no.

"And now for the treat y'all have been waiting for," Billy Bob announced. "We are going to blend the bagpipes in with the didgeridoo!"

The ensuing cacophony made Clare think of the bombing of Pearl Harbor, air-raid sirens and all. As it reverberated and resonated throughout the minuscule room, it was all she could do to sit there and not scream. This was Mike's idea of music? She glanced over at his profile, and he seemed to be smiling away, enjoying the show every bit as much as she hated it. Until, that is, he started to cough.

A horrible, racking, uncontrollable, death-defying cough. He turned such a frightening shade of red, Clare wondered if she should attempt the Heimlich maneuver on him.

Mike hoped the cough was convincing. It was either cough or laugh. He chose to cough. At least this way, he wouldn't be hurting Clare's feelings by laughing at the music she apparently loved so much.

Reaching around, Clare patted him on the back and leaned toward him. "Are you all right?" she shouted into his ear in an attempt to be heard above World War II.

He nodded, tears streaming down his cheeks.

"Mike," Clare yelled, deciding that this could be the perfect opportunity to get the heck out of Dodge. "Maybe we should go?"

Thank heavens, Mike thought, nodding gratefully at her. Yes. Go. Good.

Grabbing Clare by the hand, he stood, and without a backward glance, practically dragged her out of the room.

4

The ringing in Mike's ears had finally stopped by the time they arrived at a small Mexican restaurant that overlooked the bay. They'd both agreed it would be a good idea to take a cab, since it was getting late. He'd insisted. After all, walking this late at night could be dangerous, he'd argued. And thankfully Clare had agreed.

She really was noble minded, he thought, leaning back against the comfortable seat of the booth they shared. She didn't seem in the least bit concerned that they'd had to miss the rest of the concert.

Twirling the umbrella from his piña colada between his fingertips, he studied her in the dim glow of the restaurant's moody light. Her shiny blond hair had dried into curly ringlets around her lovely face, and her sapphire eyes sparkled and danced. As she took a tentative sip of her drink, he noticed that she made a funny little face.

"Is it okay?" he asked, inclining his head toward the blended concoction.

Clare smiled and—taking a large swig—nodded, certain that if she liked piña coladas, this would be an excellent one. However, teetotaler that she was, it was hard to say. "Yes, thank you," she said, and holding her breath, took another big gulp just to prove it. She blanched. Should she just confess and get it over with? She detested pineapples.

No, she decided, *apparently he loved them.* She could tell him some other time. If there was some other time. Shivering as the liquid burned a molten trail into her empty stomach, she tried to think of a way to get rid of the drink without seeming ungrateful.

Mike nodded magnanimously and held his glass up to her in a toast. "To the didgeridoo and bagpipes, too."

"To the didgeridoo," she echoed, and took another swig of the sickeningly sweet pineapple drink. Shuddering involuntarily, a tiny "gaaack" escaped past her lips before she could stop it.

"Are you sure you're okay?"

Clare nodded brightly and forced herself to finish her drink. "Fine," she chirped, grimacing. Which was true, now that she was almost finished with the disgusting piña colada.

"Maybe you should see the doctor about that cough of yours," Mike suggested, looking at her with concern. "It must be pretty painful."

Clare burned with embarrassment. She was going to throttle Eva. Between Puddin's nasal blockage and her own gagging over the flavor of pineapple, Mike most likely thought she wasn't long for this world. "No need, really," she assured him. "It's just—" she groped for an explanation for her pained expressions "—I think that my forty-eight-hour bra just hit its forty-ninth hour." She giggled. Goodness, she hadn't meant to confess that particular tidbit.

Arching an inquisitive eyebrow, Mike's eyes darted low, to inspect her claim. A slow smile stole across his face, causing Clare's embarrassment to escalate. Squirming uncomfortably in her chair, she wondered what was wrong with her. Her cheeks felt positively numb. And she suddenly had the crazy urge to climb up over the top of the table into Mike's lap. He was so beautiful. So beautiful it made her want to cry with the beauty of it all.

Much to Mike's delight, a wandering band of Mexican minstrels roved from table to table and played for the enjoyment of the patrons. *Good,* he thought, *more exotic music.* This was great.

"Thank you for the concert, too," she added, searching for something flattering to say. Something that wouldn't hurt his feelings about his deplorable choice for tonight's entertainment. "I learned a lot about the didgeridoo." Yes, she thought giddily as she swallowed the laughter that surged into her throat, she'd learned that the bagpipes and the didgeridoo were a lethal combination.

She'd also learned that Mike Jacoby attracted her like no other man had ever attracted her before. And she'd learned that she'd like to learn more.

"You know," she said, tilting her head at him and boldly appraising him through her heavy lids, "I don't believe I know what you do for a living."

At that moment Mike didn't know what he did for a living, either. If she kept looking at him in that sexy, unguarded way, he wouldn't be able to remember his name. "I, uh, own a garage. For foreign cars. Seattle Import Repair."

"Really?" She leaned forward, eager to know more. "Is it a family business?"

"No." Mike laughed, thinking how aghast Priss would be at the idea of working with him in a family business. "I bought it several years back, after I made a few dollars on a real estate investment. My sister sells real estate, and she gave me some good advice."

How incredibly smart he was. "The sister who sent you in to buy the suit?" Clare asked, thinking she should send this woman a thank-you note.

"Yes. She's two years older than me, but she likes to act like she's my mother."

Clare giggled. Smart and funny. He was very, very funny. "Any brothers?"

"Yes. Three. Ryan, Barry and Landon. They're all married with children, and live here in the Seattle area. Priscilla is my only sister. Dad's little princess." He watched as she ran her straw lightly against her lower lip.

"You're lucky," she murmured. A look of longing flashed across her face as she took another sip of her drink. She winced.

"You're an only child?"

She nodded. "Yes." Unless, of course, he counted Puddin'. She knew Eva did. "I always wanted a whole bunch of brothers and sisters to play with. But my mother never seemed to stay married long enough to any of her husbands to produce a sibling for me. Sometimes it was kind of lonely. I guess that's why someday I'd like to have a whole bunch of kids of my own." Casting her eyes down at the tabletop, she wondered why she was suddenly telling everything from the status of her bra to the sorrows of her past.

"Big families are fun," he agreed. "Although being the youngest can be kind of a pain. Priss still bosses me around on a pretty regular basis."

He noticed she'd finished her drink, so he signaled the waiter to bring her another one. If she liked piña coladas, by golly, he'd make sure she got them. Something about her sweet, rather lonesome expression when she spoke of her youth made him want to take care of her. Do things for her. Maybe he couldn't do anything to fill the void of an isolated childhood, but he could certainly try to make her happy in the here and now. Hell, the way she was looking at him—through those drowsy, liquid blue eyes of hers—if she asked him to hang the moon higher in the sky, he'd go get a ladder.

He wanted to know everything about her. All of her likes and dislikes—everything that her note to him hadn't said. Unfortunately the wandering minstrels finally arrived at their table and played a rousing ditty.

"Thank you." He nodded and hoped he was demonstrating his appreciation of exotic music. Slipping the guitar player a ten, he turned back to Clare. "So, tell me..."

Taking his generous tip as a request for more, the band struck up another festive number. Mike smiled gamely and nodded, willing them to leave. He'd had enough exotic music for one night. He wanted to talk to Clare. *"¡Muchas gracias!"* he said when they finished. "Feel free to go...."

"De nada." The guitar player grinned and, tapping his foot, motioned for the group to follow his lead. *"Uno, dos, tres,* go!" And once more they were noisily serenaded for what seemed an eternity to Mike.

Clare clapped enthusiastically as they finished—much to the delight of the entertainers—hoping to prove to Mike that she was open to any musical curveballs he may toss her way. Finally, to their mutual relief, the wandering minstrels wandered away.

"So," Mike began, attempting to resume their conversation where they'd left off, "why is it that you haven't started on that big family yet?" He leaned back so the waiter could straighten their table and leave Clare a fresh piña colada.

Gracious, she thought, doggedly sliding the new piña colada in front of her. She had to pretend to like another one of these revolting drinks? On an empty stomach to boot? Smiling bravely in thanks for his generosity, she began to work on the second drink. With a valiant effort, she managed to keep her facial expressions normal. She hoped.

Glancing at the fern that sat on the windowsill next to their table, she decided when the time was right, she could lose the offensive cocktail. She would just have to make very, very, very sure that Mike wasn't looking.

Then again, why kill a perfectly good fern? She could just ask for a doggy bag. If Mike asked, she could tell him that she was saving it for later. Lordy, where were all these ridiculous thoughts coming from? Plucking the umbrella out of the glass, she tossed it aside and grinned.

"Because," she said, and suddenly frowned thoughtfully as she attempted to remember what the question was, "the guy who was supposed to be their father decided he'd rather play cops-and-robbers than play house." She sighed sadly. "Beau was a cop. Not a robber." She giggled.

Mike loved the way her lilting laughter made him feel. How on earth was this Beau guy ever able to walk away from a woman like Clare? he wondered. Unless he didn't like walking in the rain or piña coladas or exotic music. Although, however annoying these little idiosyncrasies might be, they certainly weren't worth walking away from a relationship with her. "You were engaged?"

"Mmm-hmm," she hummed.

She pulled the straw from between her lips. The lips he was dying to kiss. "Ah," he commented, trying not to seem too snoopy.

"Until about three weeks ago."

"I'm sorry." He was elated.

"Don't be. My mom is sorry enough for all of us. She really liked Beau. He was her kind of man. In fact—" she giggled again and pointed her straw at him "—I think Eva may have cared more for him than I did. What about you?" she asked, feeling suddenly brave enough to quiz him. "Why aren't you married?"

"The women in my life all seemed to want to spend their lives traveling around the world. Which, I suppose, is fine when it's just the two of you. But I want kids. And a house. And my business."

Clare smiled at him through the warm glow that the piña colada had suffused her with. Thank heavens they had that much in common. She had no desire to spend her life traveling around the world, either. Kids and a house and a business sounded like a little bit of heaven to her. Perhaps she could overlook his penchant for blended pineapple drinks, his questionable taste in music and his fetish for walking in the rain, she thought hazily.

As she sat regarding him, she could see the beginnings of a five-o'clock shadow, and practically had to sit on her hands to keep from reaching across the table and touching his cheek. She was feeling inordinately bold, she realized, and decided that it would really be a bad idea to tell him how beautiful his hair was, so thick and dark, and how sexy his eyes were and how kissable his lips . . .

Mortified at the path her thoughts were taking, she shook her head and changed the subject. "So, where do you live?" she asked, proud at her offhanded tone of voice.

"I have a little place over by Lake Washington."

"Really? I don't live far from there." Leaning forward, she discovered that they were practically neighbors.

For the rest of the evening, they discussed their favorite haunts in the area, regaled each other with tales of their families, childhoods, job histories and a host of other topics that they—thankfully—seemed to have in common.

Yes, Clare thought, watching Mike's animated face as he described the three mechanics that worked for him, in spite of everything, he was a wonderful man.

* * *

Mike pulled to a stop in front of the old Queen Anne–style house where Clare lived, near the University of Washington. Leaping out of his foreign sports car, he trotted around to the passenger side, opened the door for her and assisted her to the sidewalk.

Much to her relief—and the relief of her blistered feet—he'd invited her to take a cab from the restaurant back to Monaco's. And after the fortune he'd spent on piña coladas for her, he'd insisted on playing designated driver. He was so sweet.

"This is the place," she murmured, clutching his arm as he led her to her front door. Squinting into the depths of her purse, she searched for her house keys under the dim glow of the street lamp. "Ah," she whispered, and held the elusive keys up triumphantly. "Would you like to come in for a cup of coffee?" She hoped so. Even though at least half of her drinks had gone toward watering the fern, she was still feeling a little unsteady on her feet.

Mike hesitated. As much as he knew they could both use a head-clearing dose of java, he didn't want to push his luck. The evening had gone so beautifully. At least the part at the Mexican restaurant had. He didn't want to spoil his chances of another date with her. And the way he was suddenly feeling, as he looked down into her hopeful eyes, he knew that going inside with her would probably be a bad idea. He'd never felt the need to kiss anyone the way he felt the need to kiss Clare.

"Uh...I, uh, no thanks," he declined regretfully. "I should probably get going." He always hated this part of the evening. Wondering what his date expected of him by way of a goodbye.

"Oh, sure." Clare nodded and wondered if he would try to kiss her good-night. She hated this part of the evening. It was always so awkward. "Thank you for a very...interesting and, uh, educational evening. I had a great time." Which was true, she reflected, if she didn't count walking in the rain. Or the concert. Or the piña coladas.

"Me, too." His deep, unfathomable gaze had her wondering what he was thinking.

"Well—" she turned and inserted her key into its lock, then turned back to smile up at him "—thanks again." She held her hand out to him.

Ever so slowly Mike reached out and took her hand in his. The gesture was simple, but her reaction was anything but. Heart pounding, she felt his warm, strong fingers twine with hers as he pulled her into his arms.

He held her close for a moment, in a friendly hug, and she could feel the hard, masculine planes of his body come into contact with her more pliant curves, causing a tiny whirlwind of delight to skim down her spine. Just as she began to give in to the electric warmth that turned her knees to jelly, he pulled back slightly. *Where was he going?* her brain protested muzzily, and then knew as his mouth sought hers.

His kiss, soft and exploratory at first, then increasing in pressure and demand, made up for the excruciating miles in the rain. Made up for the dilapidated Armory building. Made up for the air pollution he called music. Yes, even made up for the pineapple cocktails. Suddenly, it was all worth it. Suddenly, the entire evening was just a glorious series of events leading to this moment. A moment that, in her mind, would remain frozen in time, forever.

Cupping her face with his hands, he pulled back for an instant and, looking at her with a mixture of surprise and stark desire, hesitated only a moment before pulling her mouth back to his. Shifting in his arms, she slid her hands over his chest, beyond his shoulders and clasped them at the nape of his neck. Her mouth moved beneath his, exploring, discovering this new and incredibly exciting side of the multifaceted Mike Jacoby.

He smelled faintly of scented soap, mothballs—most likely left over from the Armory—and delightful aftershave. He tasted of piña coladas, and on him, a pineapple had never tasted better. He felt so wonderful, cradling her in his strong embrace, she knew that somehow, despite their differences, they were right for each other.

Moaning, she returned his kiss—a kiss that was far more drugging than the cocktails he'd bought for her—with reckless abandon and she was thankful for the support of his arms at her waist.

"Ah, Clare," he whispered raggedly against her cheek as he held her close, struggling for control.

Her name had never sounded so sweet.

Kissing her soundly one last time, he took a step back. "Thank you," he said sincerely, "for a truly memorable evening." He knew he had to leave now. While he still could.

"I should be the one thanking you," she murmured, "for everything."

"I'll call you?"

"Yes," she breathed, daring to hope that this wasn't just a platitude designed to help him make good his escape. "Please do," she urged. Maybe next time they could do something fun.

Backing up, his hand slid down her arm, trailing to her fingers, where it lingered for a moment before he winked lazily at her. "Soon," he promised. And with that, he turned into the night.

Monday morning, while they shared a cup of coffee in the storeroom of the men's department at Monaco's, Clare described her date with Mike to Lucy and Henri. They listened with rapt attention and howls of laughter. From time

to time they exchanged furtive, amused glances that only
served to cement Clare's fear that Mike wouldn't be back.

"I just know he's not going to call me again," Clare
moaned, allowing her head to fall dramatically against the
back of her chair. "I must have looked like I'd barely sur-
vived the *Titanic* from the moment we stepped outside.
Also, I bet he thinks I was really ignorant, not knowing what
a didgeridoo is... I could tell by the way he looked at me
when I asked. And then there were the endless piña coladas
he thinks I drank. I must look like a real lush." She cringed.
"I think he only had one of the darn things the entire evening!"

Lucy and Henri laughed till the tears streamed down their
cheeks.

"Oh, shut up." Clare hid her face in her hands. "You
guys aren't making me feel any better. It's just that—" she
propped her chin in her palm and stared dreamily into space
"—in spite of his strange ideas of a good time, I like him so
much. I'd really love to go out with him again." She'd like
to sample at least one more of those celestial kisses.

Slapping their thighs, Lucy and Henri gasped for air.

Clare narrowed her eyes at her idiotic co-workers. "Don't
you guys have some bed you could be rolling around in?"
she groused. Really, they could be more sensitive. She was
suffering here—couldn't they see that?

"I'm sorry, *ma chérie.*" Henri sobered for a moment.
"Please. Tell me the part about your panty hose again." His
handsome face scrunched beyond recognition, he hooted,
and Lucy joined in, both clutching their sides in pain.

A tiny grin threatened the corners of Clare's mouth. She
had to admit, now that she was inside where it was warm
and dry and wearing comfortable clothes, it was kind of
funny.

* * *

"How'd it go on Friday night?" Sam asked curiously as he led Bart and Roger over to the break table where Mike sat, staring off into space.

"You're fired," Mike snapped, and reached for his morning cup of coffee.

"That bad, huh?" Sam shook his head sympathetically.

"Your brother-in-law sure has some weird damn taste in music," Mike sighed, morosely eyeing his three mechanics. "If you want to know what the bagpipes and didgeridoo sound like in concert, go rev that 280Z with the broken muffler up and throw your toolbox across the room."

"Man." Sam's eyes were wide with wonder.

"Yeah. Man." Mike sighed again.

Sam tugged at his beard. "Think she'll go out with you again?"

"Hell, I don't know." He shrugged. "She seemed to enjoy herself. I just don't know if I can live through another date with her. Walked for twenty blocks in that rainstorm. My feet feel like a couple of Big Macs." Turning, he grinned at his audience. "But, man, can she kiss. Made up for a lot, I can tell you that."

"When do we get to meet her?" Bart wanted to know.

Mike snorted. "Never."

"Aw, c'mon," Roger protested.

"No way. This gal has class. I'm keeping her away from you lecherous dogs." He hadn't been able to sleep a wink Friday night, thinking about Clare in the rain, Clare in the dim glow of the restaurant and, most of all, Clare in his arms.

Bart wiggled his eyebrows. "Sounds to me like you're hooked."

"Nah," Mike denied. "But I wouldn't mind getting a little closer, if you know what I mean."

"Well, if you want to get tickets to the Medieval Country Fair this coming weekend, you'd better hurry," Bart advised, referring to Clare's list on the note Mike had found in his suit pocket. "My kids go to that dumb thing every year, and as far as I know, it's almost sold out. Both days."

"Both days?"

"Yeah. It's a weekend deal. The kids usually bring the motor home and invite a bunch of their friends. But you could probably get a room at a bed and breakfast or something. It's too far to come all the way back to Seattle. It's about two hours from here on some famous poet's farm. I forget his name."

"Really?" The last thing Mike wanted to do was spend an afternoon at the Medieval Country Fair, let alone an entire weekend. It sounded nearly as appealing as Friday night's unfortunate musical combination. But if it meant the possibility of getting another one of Clare's hot kisses, well . . . The part about spending the night at a bed and breakfast appealed to him, as well.

Plunging his hands through his hair, he looked resignedly at Bart and sighed. "Go call your kids. If the stupid thing isn't already sold out, have them get me a couple tickets."

Sam rubbed his greasy hands on his coveralls and stared at Mike. "Aren't you going to ask her if she wants to go first?" The gentle giant was a firm believer in treating people with equality and respect. Unfortunately this made him a target for Bart's and Roger's ridicule, and they never grew tired of giving him guff about his sensitive, feminine side.

"Nope, Sammy, old boy. If Bart can get the tickets, I'm going to call her and tell her we're going. Remember what the note said? She likes assertive guys that don't take no for an answer."

"Strange." Sam looked perplexed.

Roger grinned and lit a cigar. "Refreshing, ain't it?"

While Bart was in his office on the phone, Mike regaled Sam and Roger with stories of Friday night's date. While Sam was truly sorry about the way things had gone, Roger laughed until he feared he'd bust a gut.

As he went over the date and looked at it through the eyes of the guys that worked for him, Mike began to see things in a new light. He had to admit that maybe it wasn't all so bad. At least he'd gotten out of the house for once. And if he ever did find someone to settle down and have a bunch of kids with, no doubt he'd have to go to some pretty strange places once in a while to keep his marriage harmonious. Might as well accept that fact.

But a medieval fair? Why on earth did women enjoy these things? Why couldn't she have written that she'd like to go see the Sonics play? Or as far as he was concerned, they could just stay home and cuddle in front of a fire, eating popcorn and watching old movies. Now, *that* was his idea of a good time.

Unfortunately, when it came to women, he had a habit of picking ones that had a lust for adventure. At least Clare's adventures seemed to keep her in the greater Seattle area. That much they had going for them. And he couldn't forget their apparent physical compatibility.

"You're in luck." Bart grabbed a chair at the table and dropped into it. "The kids were able to get you a couple of tickets. Fortunately for you, two of my daughter's friends dropped out at the last minute, and she had some extras. You're going to have to make your own accommodations, though. The kids say that you'd better get on it right away. The whole darn town fills up every year for this thing."

"Go figure," Roger snorted, and blew a series of smoke rings toward the ceiling.

"I don't know," Sam mused. "It could be fun."

Roger, Bart and Mike all stared in disbelief at the furry bear of a man.

"Anyway," Bart continued, shifting his eyes to Mike, "the kids said to tell you that they were also able to get you into the raffle."

"Raffle? What raffle?" Mike asked.

"Beats me." Bart shrugged. "But, hey, you might just win something. Oh, and another thing." His grin was mischievous. "My daughter says you should pick up your costumes at Exit Stage Left—it's a costume shop downtown—this week. I guess there's a run on them or something."

"Costumes?" What the hell? Mike didn't like the sound of this one little bit.

"Don't worry, boss," Bart assured him. "The kids will reserve them for you. But my daughter says since it's so late, you will probably just have to take what she can get you."

"Okay." Mike was dubious. Wearing a suit to Priscilla's party was one thing, but wearing a costume for an entire weekend . . . Images of Clare's lips moving under his turned his cold blood hot again. What the heck, he decided. If this was what she wanted, one little weekend out of his life wouldn't kill him.

Reaching to the shelf behind him, he grabbed a copy of the Yellow Pages and found the section for bed-and-breakfast accommodations. Better get their rooms reserved. He grinned. Yeah, this could be fun after all, he thought, and jotted down several numbers.

"Monaco's men's department, Clare speaking," Clare said, and leaned back against the cash register.

"Hi."

It was Mike. His voice had a way of turning her blood to molten metal. Suddenly she could feel his hands on her cheeks, around her waist, in her hair. She gripped the phone a little tighter as her pulse suddenly leapt with excitement.

"Hi," she breathed.

"Can you talk?" he asked. His voice, deep and sensual, filled her ear and sent ripples of awareness through her.

"Yes ... it's slow," she assured him, hoping that if a customer should wander by, Lucy would come out to help.

"I had a great time Friday night," Mike said. The underlying sensuality of his words had her clutching the counter for support.

"Me, too." At least the very last part had been great, she amended to herself. "Thank you again."

Mike chuckled. "No problem. Listen, the reason I'm calling..." He paused and attempted to sound assertive. "I just happened to come across two tickets to the Medieval Country Fair, this coming weekend. I've already booked the last two rooms in town. And..." He paused to laugh, trying not to think of the exorbitant credit-card bill he'd racked up greasing more than one palm. "Believe me, that took some doing. We'll be staying at the Happy Valley Bed and Breakfast, since it's such a long drive from Seattle. And I know you wouldn't want to miss a minute of the, uh, fun."

"Oh?" Goodness. Was he asking her or telling her? Then again, after the kiss Friday night, he most likely had the correct impression that she was dying to go out with him again. And he was right. She was. Plus he'd gone to so much trouble, how could she say no? Since she didn't have any plans for this weekend, she really didn't have any reason to refuse.

"Yep. Oh, and don't worry about your costume. I've taken care of that too."

"My costume?"

"Well, yes, and mine, too. We were lucky. Exit Stage Left only had a few remaining medieval costumes to choose from, so I guess we'll have to take what we can get. I had to pull quite a few strings just to get those two. I hope that's all right with you.''

For once Lucy and Henri came off their break when they were supposed to, and meandered over to stand with Clare by the register. They made no bones about sprawling unprofessionally across the counter and eavesdropping on her conversation.

''Sure. I guess that would be fine.'' What else could she say with these two buttinskies drinking in her every word.

Mike took a deep breath and plunged ahead. Thankfully she seemed to like this whole idea. ''Why don't I swing by your house early Saturday morning, say around eight? If you make a pot of coffee, I'll bring the doughnuts. Since we have to wear our costumes to this thing, I figured we could put them on at your place.''

''Okay...'' Never before had any of her dates ever asked her to wear a costume. Mike didn't strike her as the kind of guy who would ask her to do anything he felt uncomfortable doing. And he certainly didn't seem like the kind of guy who got a kick out of wearing costumes for kinky reasons. She didn't know how she knew that about him. Just a gut feeling. So this whole medieval-costume thing was probably on the up-and-up. It was just that he had the strangest taste in things to do. Why, she wondered, couldn't he just invite her to a Sonics game, like any other guy?

Oh, well, time to expand her horizons. If she was ever going to shake her homebody stigma, and prove to Beau and Eva that she, too, could have an adventurous time now and again, she should probably just give herself up to the thrill of another chance to spend some time with Mike. No matter what they'd be doing.

''Sounds like fun,'' she said with animation. ''See you Saturday morning, then.''

As she hung up the phone, four probing eyes stared inquisitively at her.

"Who was that?" Lucy demanded.

"Mike."

"Ah," Henri said and arched an interested eyebrow at Lucy. "Michael of the didgeridoo, *non?* And—" he sidled up next to Clare "—what does he want now?"

"He, uh . . ." Clare vacillated for a moment. Should she tell them about Mike's unusual request? Oh, why not. They already knew all about the last fiasco. Besides, maybe they'd leave her alone about being such a stick-in-the-mud. "Well, it seems he wants to take me to the Medieval Country Fair this weekend."

"Really?" Lucy squealed and, jumping up and down, elbowed Henri in the ribs.

"You've heard of it?" Clare asked. She shouldn't be surprised. There weren't too many events in the Seattle area that got by Lucy.

"Oh, yes. You'll have a great time. If you don't have a costume, you can borrow one of mine," she offered helpfully.

"That's okay, Mike is getting them for us."

"He is?" Lucy was incredulous as she stared openmouthed at Henri. "Wow. I'm liking this guy better all the time."

Oh, no. Clare sighed heavily. Another bad omen.

5

Only the sound of a ticking clock and Clare's light breathing could be heard in the Victorian turret that was her bedroom. The sun's first, tentative rays peeped through the lace curtains that adorned her French-paned windows, caressing her cheeks and gently announcing daybreak. She lay motionless, sprawled in the same position in which she'd finally lost consciousness only an hour or so before. Then, with a light click, the numbers on her alarm clock flipped over. An irritating buzz filled her peaceful chamber and woke her out of a deep, dreamless sleep.

Groggily slapping off the offensive noise, she squinted at the bright red numbers. Seven a.m.? But it was Saturday. The day she was supposed to sleep in.

Oh, yes, she suddenly remembered, bolting upright in bed. The medieval fair. How could she forget that? she wondered, pushing her tangled hair out of her eyes. Probably because she'd spent the better part of the night trying to decide what to pack and worrying about impressing Mike with her knowledge of the event.

Lucy had helped her make a series of flash cards to aid in her study of medieval heraldry. This time she was going to make sure she knew her stuff when out on a date with Mike. She wasn't going to let him catch her with her proverbial knickers down again. Maybe she didn't know her didgeridoo from a didgeridon't, but ask her about knights in shining armor, and well—she grinned to herself—she'd be able to tell him a thing or two.

Grabbing her flash cards off the nightstand, she tossed back her comforter, hopped out of bed and padded to her bathroom. Loading her toothbrush with toothpaste, she looked at her reflection in the mirror and began to practice inserting her newfound knowledge into everyday conversation.

"Mike," she burbled past the suds in her mouth, "thank you for helping me with my coat. Speaking of coats, did you know—" she rinsed and spit "—did you know that coats of arms were at first used only by kings and princes? Yes. It's true. Then by great nobles, and by the thirteenth century—" she flipped through the cards until she found the one she was looking for "—lesser nobility, knights and even peasantry." She beamed at herself in the mirror and, for good measure, practiced batting her lashes. No, she'd skip the eyelash batting, she decided. Looked as if she had something in her eye.

"Let's see," she murmured, turning on the bathtub's faucet and pouring a little bubble bath into the stream. As she stood waiting for the tub to fill, she again went over the cards referring to European medieval armies. How on earth did Lucy keep all this stuff straight? she wondered. Between Arthur and the Anglo-Saxon wars, and the Scottish and Welsh wars...it was all just so confusing. Well, hopefully Mike would stick to the basics.

Once the tub was full, she pulled her pj's off over her head and stepped into the hot, bubbly, scented water, settled down and closed her eyes. "Ulrich von Lichtenstein, died 1275," she whispered, and hoped she was pronouncing *Ulrich* correctly. What exactly was an Ulrich? "Ooolrich. Uhlrick. Aahhhhuuulrieeech?'' she said, practicing aloud. With a German accent? She shook her head impatiently. Maybe she should forget about him.

Henri had been full of information about the Hundred Years' War. Too bad she couldn't remember any of it. Unless she counted knowing that Bertrand du Guesclin died in 1380.

Oh dear, she thought, staring morosely through the steam at the mishmash of information. She was never going to be able to remember any of this. Especially considering how nervous she got when she thought about trying to impress him as he watched her with those velvety, dark eyes of his. Frantically she flipped back and forth through the cards till they grew soggy from the bathwater and the ink started to run.

No, she sternly told herself, tossing the cards in a mushy lump on the floor and reaching for a towel, this was not the time to start hyperventilating. There would be plenty of time for that later.

As she stood toweling off, the doorbell rang.

"Oh, no," she squeaked, turning in a series of frenzied circles and searching for her clean underthings and robe. Mike wasn't supposed to be here yet. It was too early. It was only seven-thirty. She didn't have a speck of makeup on, not to mention clothes. Her hair wasn't dry. She couldn't let him see her like this.

The doorbell rang again.

She sighed. Apparently she had no choice. Clare stopped spinning and caught her breath. "Just a minute," she called, and slipped her bathrobe on over her still-wet body. She was suddenly aware that she needed a much bigger, heavier bathrobe. This one barely concealed a thing. Why hadn't she noticed that before? Exhaling noisily in resignation, she wrapped her head in a towel and hurried toward the living room. Pulling the door open, she found Mike standing on her front porch next to a stack of cartons and holding a box of doughnuts.

Mike felt as though his smile had flash frozen to his face.

Man, he thought, gaping at Clare, all pink and squeaky clean, fresh from her bath. She looked exactly the way he'd pictured in his dreams. Valiantly he tried to appear nonchalant and force some words past the wad of gauze that had suddenly become his tongue.

"Hi," he managed to say as he thrust the doughnut box into her arms and reached for his cache. "Sorry I'm so early. But," he explained, squeezing past her into her sunny living room, "I got to looking at your costume and figured maybe you could use some extra time putting it on. It looks—" he paused, unable to tear his eyes away from her as she stood smiling at him "—kind of...complicated. And as you know, they won't let us in unless we're in costume."

"Oh, I...well, uh, yes," she replied hesitantly.

He'd never seen anyone look so radiant. So beguiling, so beautiful, so—his heart thundered violently in his chest— alluring. And all without a speck of makeup or hair spray. Priscilla would hate her.

"Good idea," she said, suddenly filled with apprehension about the costume in question, and led him to her quaint, old-fashioned kitchen, where she deposited the doughnuts on her counter. "I haven't had time to make coffee yet, but it will only take a minute." She turned around to find him peering over her shoulder into her cupboard. "I, uh..."

Gracious sakes. What had she been going to say? He was standing so close, she could smell the familiar scent of his after-shave, feel his warm breath as it tickled her cheek, see the tiny gold flecks in the navy blue sea of his eyes, but she couldn't for the life of her remember what she'd been about to say. Images of their heated kiss after the concert a week ago marched disobediently into her mind, causing a liquid heat to coil through her stomach. She tightened the sash to her robe.

They stood, mere inches apart, staring at each other for a moment, and Clare was sure that the steam they generated between them could have set off the smoke detector. Clearing her throat, she gestured stupidly toward the coffee maker, which sat directly behind him. ''I'll just get the pot there,'' she said, then pondered the best way to do this as she stood transfixed, studying his impressive torso.

Mike was dressed in faded, formfitting blue jeans and a well-worn plaid flannel shirt. Over that lay a beat-up old leather jacket, which through the years had become as soft and pliant as a favored pair of slippers. The casual attire hung perfectly on his rugged frame, giving him a lazy air of virility that had Clare's pulse throbbing violently in the hollow of her throat.

She swallowed.

''Why don't I make the coffee,'' he suggested helpfully, ''and you go dry your hair? Then we can...get dressed...after, you know, you're done.'' *Oh, man*. She was turning him into a blithering idiot.

''Okay,'' she agreed, and scuttled quickly out of the kitchen. ''The coffee's in the canister on the counter,'' she called from the bathroom just before turning her hair dryer on.

As he measured the grounds into the filter, he tried to visualize her wild hair blowing in the dryer's hot breezes. He groaned. Brother, his libido was already in trouble, and they hadn't even left town yet. Even as he tried to control his wayward thoughts, he couldn't help but hope she would need some assistance putting her costume on. From what he could tell, it really did look pretty complicated.

When the coffee had finished perking, he poured her a cup and, grabbing the box with her outfit, went to the bathroom door and tapped lightly. "Clare?"

Cracking the door, she smiled out at him. "Yes?"

"I brought you some coffee, and, uh, thought I'd bring your costume to you. I hope it fits." She looked fantastic. Free flowing and curly, her hair looked like spun gold. And her lips, now a pale pink, made him want to throw caution to the wind and see if they tasted as good as they looked. But no. He was here to take her to the fair. That's what she wanted, and that's what she'd have.

"Oh, thank you." Taking the coffee and package from his hands, she pulled them through the crack in the door.

"Do you have any place special you'd like me to change?" *For instance, in the bathroom with you?* he wanted to say.

She knitted her brows for a moment. Her bedroom was a mess. But she couldn't have him changing out there in the living room, or worse, in the bathroom with her. "Uh, go ahead and use my bedroom," she told him ruefully. "It's down the hall, there on your left."

"Thanks." Trotting to the living room, Mike grabbed his own costume and headed back to her bedroom. It looked just like her. Warm, friendly and inviting. The comforter lay in a disheveled heap on her large four-poster bed, and taking a deep breath, he forced himself to block his rather risqué mental images and concentrate on the task at hand. It felt really strange to be taking his clothes off in the room where she slept, he thought, unbuckling his belt. Once he'd stripped down to his skivvies, he dug into his carton and retrieved what appeared to be a pair of tights.

"What the hell?" he muttered. Plunging his hands deeper into the box, he retrieved the rest of his ridiculous ensemble.

Surely he couldn't be expected to wear *this*.

The dark blue tunic was covered with gold dragons, and the breastplate looked like something straight out of an MTV video. And he was positive he'd seen the headdress, complete with antlers, on Cher's head, back in the seventies. At least the sword looked somewhat masculine. Maybe he could use it to amputate the antlers, he thought with disgust and tossed it on the bed. Planting his hands on his hips, he stood shaking his head. He should stuff the whole thing back in the box and toss it out the window.

On second thought, better not. The deposit he'd put down on this getup probably wouldn't cover vandalism.

Sighing, his eyes traveled from his hairy, muscular calves, to the tights he held in his hand and then up at the ceiling. He was going to look like a first-class idiot.

Clare stared in confusion at the long, conical princess hat that spouted an assortment of colored scarves from its pointy tip, and wondered how on earth she'd fit into Mike's car after she'd pinned it on her head. Hopefully he had a sunroof. That way she could also get a tan on her impressive cleavage. For it was certainly spilling out over the top of her dress in a most astonishing fashion. Eva would be proud. All this without the benefit of a forty-eight-hour SuperBra.

She tried to sigh in despair, but only managed a pitiful gasp, as she could hardly breathe at all in the torturous under-wire bodice. Although she'd given Mike her dress size when he'd called a second time Monday, the old-fashioned getup seemed too small. Too bad she couldn't hide in the bathroom for the rest of the weekend, she thought, leaning against the sink and trying to take in some much needed oxygen. But unfortunately she'd agreed to this folly, and being a woman of her word, she'd see it through to the end. If Mike enjoyed medieval pageantry and country fairs, then for his sake she would throw herself into the spirit of the thing, even if it killed her.

Wouldn't everyone be proud if they could see how adventurous she'd become? she wondered as she inspected her appearance in the full-length mirror that hung at the back of her bathroom door. She looked like a fool. People actually paid money to put themselves through this hell? Why? Surely a simple trip to the movies could be just as much fun. And much more comfortable. Valiantly she tried to stretch the stiff fabric of her dress up over her breasts. One false move and it would all be over, she thought, mortified.

Oh, well, couldn't hide in here all day. She could hear Mike thumping noisily around in her living room. He was probably anxious to get started. Might as well face the music, she thought, and opened the bathroom door.

"Hi," she called shyly before she spotted Mike. Fire stole into her cheeks, and she couldn't be sure, but she feared that even her cleavage was blushing.

Stepping into the living room where Mike stood waiting, she suddenly found herself rooted to the floor. Good heavens, she recoiled and screamed, her bosom heaving from fright. What on earth was he wearing on his head?

"Uh, hi," Mike said, turning unsteadily on his feet to face her. These pointy medieval, leprechaun-type shoes would take some getting used to. He hoped she didn't get the urge to walk any great distance today. Carefully balancing his headdress, he angled his head toward her. "Sorry, I didn't mean to scare...you." He stopped cold and stared.

Wow. His eyes darted from her bustline to her face, back to her bustline to her dress and finally back to her bustline.

She was magnificent. Maybe Bart's kids were on to something here. Maybe this costume thing wasn't so bad after all.

Who was he kidding? he wondered as his helmet slid forward over his eyes. Pushing it back up where it belonged, he grinned self-consciously and prayed he was living up to her expectations. Then he planted his hands on his hips and tried to affect a confident stance. A pose that hopefully said, *Hey, I love living on the edge.*

"How about a doughnut?" He gestured grandly to the kitchen with his sword.

"Sounds good," she chirped. Although where she would put food remained to be seen. Moving as quickly as the tightly laced bodice of her dress would allow, she followed him to the kitchen.

Clare didn't have much experience when it came to men in tights. However, interestingly enough, she thought as she studied his powerful thigh muscles, on Mike they somehow looked rugged. It was surprising, but the strange outfit served only to enhance his devastating sex appeal. His new look called to mind macho men in the ilk of Robin Hood or Errol Flynn or any number of historical swashbuckling types. Really, she mused, in a way it was too bad that men today had to wear such lackluster, drab-colored outfits. She wouldn't mind more formfitting styles for the nineties man at all. He had great legs, and from what she could see through the slits in the tunic, a very attractive derriere.

"Plain or sprinkles?" he asked.

"Oh, uh..." Dragging her eyes away from the intriguing flaps at the back of his tunic, she peered into the box he held up for her. In keeping with the spirit of adventure, she opted for the sprinkles. "Thanks for bringing breakfast," she said, grateful that they didn't have to go out for their morning meal in this garb. "I'd invite you to sit down, but I don't think either of us would be able to get back up again." She giggled as one of his antlers caught a kitchen towel and accidentally flung it across the room.

"Oh, sorry." Mike grinned and, working his way clumsily across the kitchen, snagged the towel with the toe of his medieval booty and flipped it up into his hand. "M'lady." Coming back to where she waited, he bowed awkwardly and extended the towel to her.

"My prince," Clare said demurely.

As she reached for the towel, Mike, instead of letting go, used it to pull her toward him. He studied her for a moment with an unfathomable look in his eyes, and Clare felt the gooseflesh rise on her arms. The motor in her refrigerator suddenly stopped whirring, and they stood in silence, regarding each other, listening only to the sound of their shallow breathing. Somewhere outside, a dog barked.

"You look so...beautiful," he breathed, finally breaking the silence. "Just like a real, you know, princess or something."

As he dropped his hand from the towel, Clare clutched it to her breast in a vain attempt to still her pounding heart. "Thank you," she murmured. "You look pretty fetching yourself." Her tongue glanced across her lips as she lifted her eyelashes.

"Ah, well, around the garage, I think I'll stick to my coveralls. Although," he teased, his expression somewhat bedeviling, "these antlers might come in handy as a tire iron or maybe a jack."

Clare giggled, glad at least that he didn't take himself too seriously. It certainly made his eclectic taste in things to do on a date a little more tolerable. Lifting the colorfully sprinkled doughnut to her lips, she nibbled at it and tried to think of a way to insert a historical tidbit from the flash cards into their conversation. Unfortunately she was thwarted by the sound of her mother's voice as she let herself into the house.

"Clare?" Eva called from the living room. "Clare, darling, you really should lock your front door. Why, anyone could just come barging in . . ."

Clare closed her eyes in resignation. Yes, for once she would have to agree with her mother. But it was too late.

"Oh. Hi . . ." Eva said, her eyes wide with wonder as she took in the amazing sight before her. Puddin' bobbed haplessly under her arm. "Am I interrupting something?" A smile spread across her face, and she looked pointedly at Clare, her voice loaded with meaning.

"No, Mom. We were just on our way to the Medieval Country Fair." She gestured at Mike. "Mom, this is Mike Jacoby. Mike, this is my mom, Eva Allen." She looked apologetically at him, hoping he didn't think she'd planned this meeting.

Mike removed his headgear, set it on the counter and smiled engagingly at Eva. "Pleased to meet you," he said, stepping forward and grasping her hand.

"Likewise." Eva beamed, her eyes roving unabashedly over his imposing physique. "You know," she said thoughtfully, "you kind of remind me of Kevin Costner in that Robin Hood movie. Only I don't think he had antlers on his hat. I like it, though." Her eyes danced over to Clare. "And, darling, you look perfect. I just know you'll both have a great time. The country fair is big fun."

Clare frowned at her mother. "You've heard of it?"

"Oh, sure. Hasn't everyone?"

"So it would seem," she murmured as Eva sidled up to Mike and began pelting him with questions.

His smile was beguiling as he politely satisfied her mother's curiosity. He was so charming, Clare thought, watching him calmly field her mother's conversational curveballs. It was obvious that Eva had finally come to terms with the fact that she and Beau were through and, from the look of things, was busily being converted to Mike's camp.

Never sure what new humiliation Eva would regale him with, Clare squirmed uncomfortably and wondered how to extricate Mike from her mother's enthusiastic clutches.

"Yes, she told me about the concert." Eva nodded gaily, giving Mike's bulging bicep a playful squeeze. "You know, you're exactly what the doctor ordered for my Clare. Just what she needed. Someone with a sense of fun and adventure. I'm always telling her that. Telling her that she needs to get out of the—"

"Mom," Clare interrupted before Eva could fill Mike in on what a stodgy old goose her daughter could be, "what are you doing here?"

"Oh, yes, well, I was hoping you could take Puddin' for the weekend." Eva deposited a tender kiss on the dog's balding pate. "I have to go to a garden-club convention down in Portland this weekend, and Beatrice will be riding with me. Beatrice is allergic to fur. It's the strangest thing." Eva shook her platinum head. "She gets violently ill whenever Puddin' is around."

Clare rolled her eyes. Good old Beatrice wasn't the only one.

"Anyway," Eva continued, oblivious to her daughter's lack of enthusiasm when it came to her baby, "I couldn't find a sitter, and Puddin' refuses to be left at the kennel. Poor thing. He gets so agitated whenever I get ready to go anywhere. He can't eat and starts to shake—well, it's almost as if he knows his mommy has to go bye-bye. Sometimes I think he's afraid I might not come back." Her voice was plaintive as she murmured some soothing baby talk into Puddin's wilted ear.

"Don't worry, Mrs. Allen. Clare and I will be happy to take Puddin' along to the country fair," Mike said assertively, hoping that Eva, like her daughter, liked assertive men. After all, this was the perfect opportunity to score points with Clare's mother. It was the least he could do, he thought, dubiously inspecting the ugly mutt as it stared up at him through its small, beady black eyes. How much trouble could the little runt be?

"You will?" Eva breathed, smiling broadly with a mixture of relief and admiration.

"We will?" Clare gasped, staring dumbfoundedly first at Mike, then at Eva. Then at Puddin'.

"Sure," he grandly assured them, reaching out to pat Puddin'. The dog snarled and snapped at his hand, and Mike recoiled quickly, counting his fingers to make sure they were all still there. Maybe this wasn't such a good idea after all. He exchanged a trepidatious glance with Clare. She didn't look any more confident than he felt.

"Oh, don't worry about that," Eva said blithely. "Once he gets used to you, he's as sweet as a little teddy bear. Aren't you, Puddin'-woodin?"

"But, Mom," Clare protested. "What about his back problems? Doesn't he need his brace?" Grasping at straws, she attempted to back out of Mike's magnanimous commitment to canine day care.

Waving an airy hand, Eva said, "Oh, he's all better. I have his crate in the car, and his food and pills and brush and sweater and playpen and so on. Everything you'll need. Don't worry about a thing. You'll be fine."

After an endless number of trips from Eva's station wagon to Mike's sports car, Puddin' was finally packed and ready to go. While they accomplished this task, Clare finished her own packing. Tucking her flash cards into her purse, she quickly put her bedroom back to rights, folding

Mike's street clothes into a neat pile and setting them on her suitcase. It seemed such a wifely thing to do, she thought, coiling his belt and laying it on top of his jeans.

Dozens of different emotions, everything from dread to wild anticipation, crowded into her throat as she made her bed and tugged her comforter into a tidy square. She was going away for the weekend with Mike. And even though they would be staying in separate rooms, the very idea was incredibly intimate. Picking Mike's battle-scarred leather jacket up off the floor, she cradled it in her arms and buried her nose in its rich leather. It smelled wonderful, like him.

Sensing Eva's presence behind her, she turned to face the beaming woman.

"Oh, Mom," Clare sighed. "How could you saddle us with Puddin'? This is supposed to be a date. Not a baby-sitting service."

"Why, darling, it was his idea. He is wonderful! And the way he wears a pair of tights...he's a keeper." Eva pretended to swoon. "So hang on to him for dear life and don't let him get away like you did with Beau," she instructed, shaking her head sadly. "I'm glad to see you're making an effort this time to indulge in your man's interests. I'm proud of you."

"Mom, please," Clare groaned. Eva always had a way of making her feel like a recalcitrant child.

"Really. I mean it. I know this weekend in the country is a stretch for you. But if you give yourself up to the moment, you may just discover that you are having a good time. Mark my words."

Kissing Clare on the cheek, Eva stepped lightly out of her room, calling a cheery goodbye over her shoulder, and promised to pick Puddin' up first thing Monday morning.

* * *

By the time they finally left, Clare was nearly undone. The back seat of Mike's sporty foreign import was filled to bursting with the odious Puddin' and his accoutrements. Their own suitcases, costume pieces and other sundry belongings were squeezed in alongside, making the interior of his car seem almost unbearably familiar.

His hand brushed against her knee as he threw the vehicle into gear and tore down the road as if the hounds of hell were after him. And if Puddin's disgruntled growling was any indication, they were. Scarcely braking at the side-street stop signs, he ground from low to high speeds—causing her thigh to burn from his touch—and sailed toward the country fair. Buildings and trees were a blur as he sped from the on ramp, roared over several lanes and merged with traffic on the freeway proper.

Mike draped his hands over the top of his steering wheel and began to relax. He never felt more confident than when he was behind the wheel of a well-tuned car. Not to mention the fact that the sooner he got out of town, the less likely the chance of running into someone he knew, dressed as he was in this idiotic outfit.

Racking his brain for a topic of conversation that wouldn't reveal his ignorance on the subject of medieval country fairs, Mike opted for what he hoped was safe conversational ground.

"Your mom is great," he said, sliding an easy sidelong glance at Clare.

She smiled sheepishly. "Yes, she is. Her attachment to her dog takes a little getting used to, though." Shrugging lightly, she gestured to the back seat. "Sorry about getting stuck with Puddin'. Hopefully he'll come around."

"No problem. I'm sure, once we get there, he'll be fine."

Puddin' snorted loudly.

Mike accelerated uneasily at the sound, as if trying to outrun Eva's little bundle of joy.

"How long until we get there?" Clare asked, trying to divert the subject away from the indignant dog. At the rate they were traveling, surely they would arrive any moment. She had hoped to have some more time to study her notes. Perhaps if she angled her purse just right, she could see Lucy's flash cards and make a halfway intelligent attempt at discussing something medieval.

"Oh, Happy Valley is about a two-hour drive from Seattle. That's why I got us a couple of rooms at the bed and breakfast. I didn't want you to miss any of the action." He sent her a happy sideways grin.

"Super," she said, trying to inject a note of carefree enthusiasm into her voice for his benefit. She studied his profile in the morning sunlight. He was so handsome. She still couldn't believe her good fortune. If only they were on their way to a quiet little picnic for two in the country. Then life would be perfect. Never mind, she decided. She'd count her blessings. At least Mike wasn't asking her to jump out of a plane, or scale to the top of Mt. Rainier, as Beau, in the throes of his midlife crisis, was wont to do.

"I like your car," she told him, and could tell immediately that she'd found the way to Mike's heart.

"Thanks." His eyes crinkled as he checked his mirror and changed lanes.

For the next several miles, he chatted eagerly about the history of this particular car, and fascinated Clare with his knowledge of foreign cars in general. Impressed, she could tell that he really loved his line of work. She could tell by the animation of his expression, the twinkle in his eyes, the smile...

"Damn," he growled, glancing into his rearview mirror.

"What is it?"

"Cop," he spat through his tightly clenched jaw. Signaling, he pulled over to the side of the road and, muttering some pithy expletives, began searching though his glove box for the registration. "Sorry," he said, smiling apologetically up at Clare as he leaned across her lap. Finally finding what he was looking for, he slammed the compartment shut and sighed. "I'm going to get a ticket for sure. I know I was doing at least twenty miles over the speed limit." Reaching toward the door, he lowered his window and waited for the policeman to arrive.

Clare had to admire his honesty. Most people would be busy thinking up excuses.

"Hi, there." The officer poked his head into Mike's car and, taking in his costume, broke into an earsplitting grin. Lifting his head, he glanced from Mike to Clare, his eyes widening in shock. "Clare?"

"Hi, Beau." Clare wanted to die.

6

It was obvious that Officer Beau thought the whole situation was hilarious. And policeman or no, Mike had the foolish urge to leap out of the car with his sword and challenge the cocky, smirking lawman to some kind of showdown. However, since Clare's ex had the power to toss him into the hoosegow, Mike decided to play it cool. Keep his opinions about Beau's midlife crisis to himself.

So, he fumed, sitting silently as Beau snatched his automobile registration out of his hand, *this was the jerk that had hurt Clare.* For reasons he could only begin to guess at, Mike had an immediate and intense dislike for the swaggering, arrogant policeman. And he suspected those reasons had nothing to do with the fact that the man had pulled him over and was in the process of giving him a speeding ticket.

He glanced over at Clare to see how she was doing. Not good. She seemed distinctly rattled. For some reason, that vaguely depressed him, as he considered the possibility that Clare was still hung up on her man in blue.

Although, he thought morosely as he stared unseeing out the window, better to find out now, before he got in too deep with her. If he was going to get away with his heart in one piece, he wanted to find out exactly where he stood with her. Because as much as he hated to admit it, there was something about Clare Banning that had already gotten under his skin. Squirming uncomfortably in his seat, Mike decided that he was going to fire Bart. And Bart's kids.

Clare tried not to fidget. But it was hard. What if Beau opened his big mouth? Blew her cover about this medieval-fair thing? Beau of all people knew that she'd rather dig a swimming pool with a spoon than attend a festival in a costume. It just wasn't her kind of thing. That is . . . until Mike Jacoby had come along.

As she watched Mike search his tights for his wallet, Clare began to count her blessings that she hadn't ended up married to Beau. Sitting there, comparing the two men as the policeman waited impatiently for Mike to locate his driver's license, she wondered how she'd ever thought that Beau was her type. It was so obvious. Why hadn't she ever noticed how incompatible they were before?

Puddin' snuffled and whimpered from the back seat, reminding Clare that the real reason she'd never noticed how wrong Beau was for her, was probably because Eva had been so busy pushing them together. But now that she was away from the situation, she could more clearly see that the two men—thankfully—were really nothing alike.

Even though they both shared an adventurous spirit, Mike seemed well-grounded in the reality of everyday life, whereas Beau was consumed by wanderlust. This realization sent a thrill of liberation rippling down her spine. Mike was mature, self-confident and easygoing. Beau was immature, self-absorbed and intense. And even though Mike's idea of a good time would still take a monumental adjustment on her part, it was clear that he was more her style.

As much as she liked to place blame, she knew it wasn't Beau's fault that they weren't compatible. It wasn't anyone's fault. The freedom that she felt from this newfound knowledge was exhilarating.

Now, if she could only keep Beau from completely spoiling what promised to be an interesting, if not altogether enjoyable, weekend with Mike.

"Clare?"

Mike's agitated voice drew her out of her reverie.

"Yes?"

"Did you happen to notice my wallet anywhere at your house?" He patted his tights. "I don't seem to have it on me."

Drawing her lower lip into her mouth, she worried it between her teeth as she thought. "Do you think maybe it fell out in my bedroom when you took off your pants?"

Beau arched an arrogant eyebrow and scowled at Mike. "Out of the car, lover-boy," he ordered, dramatically yanking Mike's door open.

"Oh, for crying out loud," Mike muttered under his breath as he tried to extricate his awkward, medieval booties from the car's cramped interior.

"What's that you say?" Beau demanded.

"Nothing, Officer." Wrestling with the cumbersome breastplate, Mike finally made it to a standing position.

"You know, it's against the law to drive without your license," Beau unnecessarily informed him, walking in a slow circle around Mike, studying his costume, his mouth quirked with amusement.

Mike wanted to punch him. What on earth had Clare ever seen in this blowhard? He was like a character in a bad cop show.

"So, where were you off to in such an all-fired hurry?"

Closing his eyes tightly, Mike plunged his hands through his hair and sighed. "The Medieval Country Fair," he reluctantly informed Beau. Cars whizzed by on the freeway, honking and waving at the man in tights. Feeling naked, Mike wished someone would run over him and put him out of his misery. This had to be the single most humiliating experience of his life. And Clare was probably sitting in the car, wishing she was still engaged to Beau. Obnoxious as the policeman was, at least *he* was wearing pants.

Beau ducked his head into the driver's-side window and stared in surprise at Clare. "The Medieval Country Fair? I didn't know you went in for that kind of thing."

Clare wanted to punch him. "That's because you never asked what *I* liked to do," she snapped indignantly. Neither had Mike, for that matter, but at least Mike's idea of a good time didn't involve risking life and limb.

"My, my," Beau tsked, and grinned. "You're beautiful when you're angry." His tone was filled with the same condescending attitude she remembered. "So," he asked, his eyes glassy and focused somewhat south of her chin, "did lover-boy leave his wallet in your bedroom or not?"

Sighing in exasperation, Clare hiked her skirts up around her thighs and unceremoniously dived, bottom up, into the back seat. "I don't know," she mumbled, rifling through the pile of their belongings. "It might be in his pants pocket. We threw them in the back seat before we left."

"Really?" Beau snorted. "Clare, does your mother know what you're doing?"

Clare clamped her lips on her retort. She didn't owe Beau any explanation. "Here it is." Tossing the wallet in question at Beau, she flopped back into her seat and pointedly ignored him.

Beau strode back to the waiting police car and called in the information on Mike. Taking this opportunity, Clare forced open her door against the buffeting tail winds kicked up by the passing traffic and, struggling out of the car, made her way to Mike's side. The stiff breezes tore unmercifully at her cumbersome skirts, and the scarves that flowed from the tip of her hat whipped wildly around her face.

"I'm so sorry about all this," she yelled up at him, attempting to be heard above the roar of the freeway. Cars began to slow down to stare at the absurdly dressed pair.

"I just hope he doesn't cite me for any moving violations he thinks I may have committed in your bedroom this morning." Mike grinned down at her and, placing a light hand at her waist, led her farther away from the traffic.

Clare went pink. "He'd better not." She shot an annoyed look in Beau's direction. "My life is none of his business anymore. We are finished. Now more than ever, I'm sure of that."

Breathing a sigh of relief, Mike smiled down at her. *Hallelujah.* He still had a chance. Suddenly it didn't matter that nearly everyone in the greater Seattle area was getting an eyeful of Mike Jacoby's derriere as the passing wind lifted and dropped the back of his tunic. He was with Clare. Doing things that made her happy. Getting to know her better. And he thought as she stood beaming happily up at him, he definitely liked what he was finding.

"I still can't believe he gave us a ticket," Clare fumed as Mike guided his car—much more slowly now—down the winding road that led to the estate where the fair was being held.

Grinning, Mike reached over and squeezed her hand. "Don't worry about it. As far as I'm concerned, he's the loser in the deal."

Clare smiled bashfully at the subtle meaning of his words. He was so wonderful. It almost made the pain and suffering of their dates worthwhile. If the old axiom held true, anything worth having was worth working for. And this weekend she had her work cut out for her.

They had decided that since it was getting so late in the morning—thanks to Beau—they would go straight to the fair and check in to the bed and breakfast later in the afternoon. This was fine with Clare, as the idea of checking into a room where she would be staying under the same roof with Mike made her almost as nervous as the fair itself.

"Oh, look." She pointed out the windshield as a sign came into view. "Medieval Country Fair, Next Right." Her heart pitter-patted uncomfortably. She wasn't ready for this. Was it too late to tell him that she had a headache?

"Yeah, this must be the place." Mike nodded and, signaling his turn, proceeded to bounce across the rough grass of a field that had been converted into a temporary parking lot. Puddin' grunted indignantly as he was tossed about in his transport crate. Following the frantic gestures of a local peasant who stood in the middle of the lot, directing traffic, Mike finally lurched to a stop and cut the engine.

"We made it," Clare commented with relief as she tucked her bosom back into her dress where it belonged. Luckily Mike had parked when he had. The rough terrain of the parking lot was definitely not conducive to modesty, as her bustline seemed to be of a mind to—bust loose.

They sat for a moment, both staring off toward the horizon, taking in the intimidating array of tents, horses, knights and other various and sundry medieval pageantry. And both wondered what on earth they could say to convince the other that they were having an excellent time.

Mike was the first to break the ice. "What should we do with the dog?" he asked, reluctant to use the animal's ridiculous name.

"I guess I could carry him," Clare volunteered. "Mom never leaves him in the car. He gets these fits...." she finished lamely, wishing that her mother would stick to goldfish in the future.

"Sounds good," Mike agreed with relief, remembering the way the hound had gone after his fingers. Once again he fought his way out of the car and, coming around, assisted Clare in the same. Then, after they'd donned their headgear, stuffed Puddin' into his sweater and locked the car, they were off.

The country fair was everything both Clare and Mike were afraid it would be. Once they'd produced their tickets and made it through the guards at the gate, they entered a foreign world for which neither of them was prepared. Before they'd gone ten feet, a bard of sorts serenaded them with an off-key ode to historical and legendary events that—much to Clare's chagrin—Lucy hadn't covered in the flash cards.

Mike studied Clare's attractive profile as she smiled indulgently at the space case that caterwauled about the days of olde. *She sure likes that exotic music,* he thought. The singer reminded Mike of a nerdy little guy that he was always rescuing back in high school. But this wasn't high school, and as far as Mike was concerned, the nerd was on his own. Tugging impatiently on Clare's sleeve, he led her and Puddin', who was drooling most unattractively, away from the bard and into the milling, ostentatiously decorated throng.

"Wow. That was some singing," Mike said, searching for something flattering to say.

Boy, Clare thought, *he really likes that exotic music.* "Yes, it sure was," she agreed, following him as he eagerly explored the interesting crowd. The noise was obviously terrifying to Puddin', and he began to quiver uncontrollably in her arms.

Mike, eager to get away from the bizarre crowd, searched for a concession stand. Maybe a hot dog and a beer would make him feel a little better. As they threaded their way through the throbbing sea of humanity, they were treated to all manner of eccentric characters. Many seemed to be leftover flower children, parading around in every type of me-

dieval garb and talking loudly to each other in some sort of
affected Olde English dialect.

Everywhere they looked, people stood about, playing the
lute, drinking far too much ale and dancing some kind of
strange, ritualistic jig that neither Mike nor Clare could
identify. Men wearing full coats of armor clinked and
clanked about, some on the ground, some on horses. Flags
of all shapes and sizes flapped in the breeze against the
cloudless blue sky. On all four sides of the meadow that was
the fair site, loomed a dark, thickly wooded forest that
served neatly as a colorful backdrop for the dozens of white
tents that littered the area.

A few of the tents housed farriers and their tools for the
horses. Others housed musicians and their medieval instruments. Some served as concession and trinket stands, and
some served no purpose other than to offer shade to the
milling crowd.

A large field situated behind the tents was cordoned off
for what looked like a spectator sport. Bleachers surrounded an arena of closely clipped grass where horses
wearing very heavy, extravagantly engraved and gilded armor pranced and snorted. And off to one side, where many
of the horses were tethered, sat a crude replica of a castle,
probably at least twenty feet in height from what Mike could
tell, fashioned from concrete blocks and large pieces of
slate. Grown men frolicked and cavorted like little kids in
front of this castle, brandishing lances at each other and
pretending to joust.

He wouldn't be caught dead doing something so stupid,
Mike thought, glancing at Clare, who watched them with
what he could only guess was admiration. He'd better not
tell her what he thought of adults who played dress-up and
ran around pretending to fight. After all, he supposed, they
weren't really hurting anyone. Let them have their fun.

Mike spotted a stand where they were selling what looked like something edible. "Why don't we have a little lunch before we explore much further?" he suggested hopefully. His doughnut had worn off hours ago.

"Oh, yes. That's a terrific idea." Clare shifted Puddin' higher on her shoulder. "Why don't I save us a table, and you go get in line?" she suggested, anxious to get off her feet. What was it about going out with Mike that made her feet ache so? she wondered as she watched him forge his way through the crowd and vie for a place in line. Puddin' grew heavy in her arms, so she made her way over to an empty picnic table and set him on the ground. The poor thing wasted no time in diving under the bench.

"You want to hide?" Clare asked, peering at Eva's pet as it cowered in the shade. Fine with her.

Kicking off her princess slippers, she hitched her skirt up around her knees and, wiggling her toes in the grass, watched a juggling court jester entertain a crowd of children.

She had to admit the entire affair was rather interesting, in an otherworldly sort of way, but she was sure it would never make her top-ten list of fun things to do. Maybe someday she could convince Mike that they should go to the coast and just walk along the beach in their bare feet. It might not be a laugh a minute in the adventure category, but hey, at least their feet would survive. They could hold hands and watch the waves break over the rocks or skip stones or hunt for seashells. Maybe even share one of those sexy kisses as they sat in front of a little camp fire, roasting marshmallows and watching the sun set. She shivered at the enticing thought. Then they could go out for some clam chowder.

Mmm. Her mouth began to water. She was hungry.

"All they had were some cups of mead, crusty chunks of bread and these turkey legs," Mike said apologetically, arriving at the table moments later and handing Clare a flimsy paper plate. "It was either that or gruel."

Clare made a playful face. "Thanks. You made a wise choice." Setting her plate down on the table, she tore off a small piece of turkey and held it under the bench for the dog. Puddin' eyed the morsel skeptically and, turning up his nose, cowered farther away. Shrugging, Clare smiled at Mike. "He usually gets steak."

"Wow." Mike grinned. "I'm lucky if I get a dried-up piece of meat loaf in a TV dinner." He set his plate down beside Clare's, along with his headdress, and very carefully maneuvered himself onto the bench next to her.

"Me, too." Clare laughed, pushing her skirts out of the way to make room for his sword.

They ate in silence for a while, munching their turkey legs and crusts of bread, each longing for the comfort of the bed and breakfast and some decent food.

"I usually like my turkey with all the trimmings," Mike ventured, hoping he wouldn't offend her culinary predilection for the fair's dubious fare. "You know," he mumbled over a mouthful of the sawdust-dry, crusty bread, "like at Thanksgiving or Christmas."

"Mmm," she agreed, her eyes reflecting the deep blue of the azure sky. "I love stuffing. And cranberry sauce. And pumpkin pie."

"Yeah." Mike sighed hungrily at the tasty picture her words painted. "Do you like sweet potatoes?"

Clare nodded. "With those little marshmallows on top. I love those."

"Oh, man, that is good." Mike took a big swig of the potent mead to help wash down the bread. "And soft, hot dinner rolls, dripping with butter." Tired of wrestling with his crust, he dropped it on the table, where it landed with a thud.

She closed her eyes, and an expression of ecstasy crossed Clare's face. "Oh, I love those, too. You know—" she opened her eyes and pointed at him with her turkey leg "—I got a bread machine for Christmas. You can make really good dinner rolls with that little baby, let me tell you." She knocked on the table with her drumstick for emphasis. "Plus, pizza dough and regular bread and all kinds of stuff."

"I'll bet." Mike nodded, thinking that a pizza would hit the spot. "You ever make pizza?"

"All the time. It's easy. My favorite is Clare's combo." She lifted her eyebrows teasingly.

Mike laughed. She was so cute. "What's that?"

"It varies, depending on what I have left over in the fridge." She refrained from telling him that she hated Canadian bacon and pineapple. He might realize how much she disliked those awful piña coladas. "Sometimes pepperoni. Sometimes sausage and olives."

It sounded like heaven to Mike.

They went on to describe to each other their favorite dishes, finding that they had a host of tastes in common. Everything from Italian to Chinese cuisine, and a few of their own favorite dishes in between. From food, the topic moved to restaurants, to nightclubs, to dancing, to favorite television shows, and from there to current events, politics and religion.

How was it, Clare found herself wondering—as Mike described a political cartoon that made fun of a local politician and caused her to laugh herself silly—that they could have so many things in common, yet when it came to spending their free time, still be worlds apart?

Well, she figured, she wouldn't worry about it right now. No, right now she would concentrate on getting through the rest of the day in this miserable costume. She tossed her turkey leg on her plate, deciding that, due to the tightness of her dress, she was finished eating. No use filling her stomach with this lousy bread, either. The stays in her dress cut painfully into her sides as it was.

"Well—" Mike tossed his still half-full plate on top of Clare's "—why don't we go see what's cooking over there in the castle?" He gestured to the pile of concrete blocks and rocks over by the bleachers.

"Okay." Clare reached for her slippers.

"Where's the mutt?" Mike asked. "I'll carry him for a while if you want, and give you a rest."

"That would be...great," Clare puffed as she bent over and peered under their table. Provided they could find the mutt. Puddin' was nowhere in sight. Kicking her skirts out of the way, just in case he was hiding in the folds, she searched first under their bench, then, getting down on her hands and knees, under the benches of the surrounding tables. "Uh-oh," she moaned, crawling on all fours, as best she could, considering the volume of her skirts, "I don't see him."

"What?" Concerned, Mike joined her on the ground. "He's got to be around here somewhere," he assured her, hoping he was right. He wasn't wild about the idea of Clare's mother coming after him with blood in her eye. Not when he was trying so hard to woo her daughter.

"Here, uh, Puddin'," he called. Geez. He didn't think he could feel more idiotic than he had out there on the freeway. But here he was.

"Oh, no." Clare began to panic. "What are we going to do?" Eva would kill her if anything happened to that balding rodent she called a dog. She began to crawl rapidly from table to table, calling for the dog and hoping against hope that both Puddin' and her breasts would stay put for a moment.

Mike crawled after her and, when he wasn't busy searching for the repulsive Puddin', took time to admire the way Clare's behind swayed so fetchingly beneath her skirts. From time to time she would pause, smile up at some lunching nobility or another and, begging her forgiveness, lift her skirts and peer underneath for Puddin'.

Mike grinned. She was so damn cute.

But Puddin', rebelling at being dragged to the country fair, remained missing. Clare didn't really blame him. She'd considered running away herself. And if it wasn't for the man in the antler headdress—who seemed as genuinely distressed about the missing mutt as she was—well, she'd be outta here, too.

Mike's distress caused his blood pressure to rise like a loaf of Clare's homemade bread. When he got a hold of that dog, he was going to throttle it, he thought grimly. Standing, he followed Clare as she dashed through the crowd, calling "Here, Puddin'."

A group of peasants and nobility alike chuckled and commented about the couple as they whizzed by, chasing one another around the fair, calling each other by their darling pet name.

"Puddin'," they could be heard saying, "isn't that sweet?"

Mike wanted to stop and set them straight, but Clare was moving too fast. As it was, it was all he could do to keep from tripping over his booted feet. He finally caught up with her back at their original table.

"Mike, this is just awful," she wailed. Settling into a giant heap of fabric as he reached her, she sat on the bench and buried her face in her hands. "What are we going to do?"

Dropping down next to her, he gathered her into his arms and, cursing the unyielding breastplate, whispered reassurances into her ear. "Don't worry, I'll think of something," he told her, working the anxiety from her shoulder blades with the tips of his fingers.

And she knew he would. There was just something strong and reassuring about Mike. Even though he liked to spend his weekends wearing strange clothing at these cockamamy medieval fairs, he gave her a sense of security that she'd never had before. Somehow she knew deep down in her soul, that—unlike any of her old boyfriends, and unlike any of Eva's husbands—when the chips were down, she could count on Mike.

She sighed contentedly, resting her heated cheek on the cool metal of his breastplate, loving the feeling of his hand as he gently stroked her hair. For a brief moment, she almost found herself wishing that they lived in another place and time. A time where she was a real damsel in real distress, instead of a party pooper in search of a dog with back problems.

A razzing sound came from a clump of grass near one of the many white tents behind their table.

Clare pulled her face away from Mike's chest and looked up at him. "Is your stomach growling?"

"No." He relaxed his hold on her.

"Mine, either."

Together they made a beeline for the suspicious sound. There they found Puddin', his face buried in an empty cup of mead snoring. Mike reached out and poked him.

"I think he's drunk," he said incredulously. "He smells like a brewery."

"Drunk?" Clare rolled her head back and stared up at the sky. "Great. Just great."

"Don't worry. We have till tomorrow morning to sober him up," Mike assured her. Lips twitching, he tried to swallow his mirth.

Shooting him a beleaguered look, Clare asked, "How in heaven's name did this happen?"

Mike inclined his head at the tent closest to their table. "Mead-tasting tent." He pointed at one of the casks that had tipped over.

Puddin' snored, and Clare felt her face scrunch up with laughter. Before she knew it, both she and Mike were laughing till the tears streamed down their faces. Neither of them were sure if the tears were from the wonderful, liberating laughter that they shared, or from the fact that they still had to get through the afternoon at the Medieval Country Fair.

"Will Sir Michael Jacoby please report to the jousting table." The overhead PA system cracked and buzzed. "Sir Michael Jacoby to the jousting table."

Clare, cradling the drunken dog in her tired arms, looked quizzically at Mike. "Did you hear that?"

"Yes. I wonder what that's all about. I wonder—" he glanced around "—where the jousting table is."

They'd been walking for hours, and the fairground had become a blur to Clare. "I think I saw something like that over at the castle when we passed by." Extracting a finger out from under the dog's belly, she pointed as best she could.

Mike lifted the still-snoring Puddin' out of Clare's arms and up onto his shoulder. Touching her elbow, he motioned for her to follow him.

Clare had been right. The jousting table was directly in front of the castle.

"Hi, I'm Mike Jacoby," Mike introduced himself to the ladies and knights who manned the table.

"Oh, wonderful," a grandmotherly gal who sported a rather large crown said, adjusting her glasses and squinting at her clipboard. "Dee, he's here. Get his stuff for him, will you, dear? It's over there." She pointed behind her, then turned to beam up at Mike. "You're just in time, honey."

"For what?" Mike asked, and exchanged a quizzical glance with Clare.

"Goodness, didn't you know? You won the raffle."

"I did?"

"You sure did," Dee crowed, handing him a lance.

Mike grinned headily at Clare. At least something was finally going his way. "What'd I win?"

"Why, you get to joust in the tournament!"

Mike could hear Clare screaming above the riotous crowd from where she sat at the top of one of the many sets of bleachers. He wished someone would tell her that he was going to live. At least he hoped so. However, as he lay, sprawled out in the middle of the jousting field, feeling as if he'd just been hit by a speeding locomotive, he was beginning to wonder.

How on earth he'd ever ended up jousting in a tournament, he'd never know. As the paramedics that had been standing by slowly removed his coat of arms, he knew that his ankle would probably never be the same. Oh, well, served him right. He'd been showing off. Trying to convince Clare that he was her knight in shining armor. He should have told good old Lady Dee, over there, to give his raffle prize to the runner-up. But no, he'd had something to prove to Clare.

Dee had convinced him that it was an honor to joust. Not just anybody got the chance. No, no, no. It was a once-in-a-lifetime deal. Mike had too much pride to turn down such a challenge. Especially since Clare had looked so impressed.

Besides, he had figured, what could happen? He was wearing enough metal to build a car, for crying out loud.

Too bad that the guy that had come galloping at him full speed, wielding his lance like a golf club, hadn't known he was a beginner. If he had, maybe he wouldn't have tried to play field hockey, with Mike's head as the ball.

Once the paramedics had determined that all Mike needed was a little ice on his sore ankle and a couple of aspirin, he was hoisted onto a stretcher and carted off to the sidelines amid a wild ovation from the stands. With a momentous effort, Mike lifted his throbbing head and waved weakly at the crowd.

7

"I'm coming, I'm coming, dammit! Just keep your blasted pants on."

Mike jerked his hand away from the front-desk bell as though it were scalding hot and exchanged a perplexed glance with Clare. The proprietor of the Happy Valley Bed and Breakfast—who yelled at them from somewhere behind yonder door—sounded anything but happy. Leaning against the giant mahogany desk, Mike attempted to take some of the pressure off his swollen ankle as he waited to be checked in to the ramshackle old farmhouse turned inn. He rubbed his pounding temples and tried to smile at Clare. Great time to feel like hell.

"How do you feel?" she whispered, and gave his aching bicep a squeeze.

Sliding her hands up to his neck, she gently rubbed the tension from between his shoulder blades.

"Fine," he lied, loving the feel of her skillful hands on his poor, beat-up muscles. Maybe when they got to their rooms he could play on her sympathy and get her to give him a back rub. And an ankle rub. And a foot rub. *Oh, man, yeah,* he thought, allowing his head to loll back against her probing fingers, *a foot rub.* He, of course, would be only too happy to return the favor....

"Hey, knock that off," a frumpy, frowzy woman wearing a Hello, I'm Mrs. Griswold name tag over her torn and faded bathrobe commanded as she slogged into the room. Her tiny, lightning-quick eyes flashed suspiciously at them, while her ferretlike nose and lips twitched with ill humor. She stood, slumped under the weight of her numerous pink sponge-curlers, arms planted firmly on her generous hips, taking in with disdain their medieval costumes.

Clare awkwardly dropped her hands from the back of Mike's neck.

"Are you married?" Mrs. Griswold barked her question, the furrow between her brows deepening. At their negative response, she pointed an accusatory finger at them. "We got rules around here, at the Happy Valley Bed and Breakfast," she growled. "And that includes no hanky-panky if you're not married. Not under my roof. Got that?" she snapped as the front-desk phone rang.

Mike turned slightly toward Clare. "She doesn't want to be the only one not having any fun," he muttered under his breath as Mrs. Griswold snatched the phone off the wall and proceeded to read some poor guest the riot act.

Clare bit her lip and nodded, her eyes twinkling into his.

Slamming the phone into its cradle, the crotchety clerk swung around to face them. "Name?"

"There should be two rooms under Jacoby."

The older woman checked the guest ledger. "Yeah. Got 'em here." Mrs. Griswold filled out their paperwork, had Mike sign several documents, then carefully compared his handwriting to that of his driver's license and credit card. Finally she grabbed a couple of keys off the wall and tossed them on the desk. "I meant what I said about the rules. No loud music. No cooking in the rooms. Absolutely no pets of any kind. Got that?"

Mike nodded, glad that they'd decided to leave the still-inebriated Puddin' asleep in the back seat of his car.

"And—" Mrs. Griswold slapped the front desk with the palm of her hand for emphasis "—I go to bed by 9:00 p.m. every night. So if you need anything, you'd better ask me before nine, because after that, you're outta luck. I hate the weirdos that the medieval fair brings to town every year," she crabbed, staring pointedly at the antler headdress Mike held under his arm. "I don't need that kind of business. So behave yourselves, or I'll be only too happy to throw you out on your ears."

Mike picked the keys up off the desk and nodded amiably at Mrs. Griswold. "Thank you," he rasped, and smiled as charmingly as he could through the twinges of pain that shot through his ankle. "Have a nice day."

Mrs. Griswold, who wore her foul temper like a thorny crown, ignored his pleasantries. "Don't lose those keys," she called after them as Mike—anxious to get away before she turned them in to "America's Most Wanted"—ushered Clare toward the exit and their carload of personal effects.

Resting a light hand at Clare's waist, Mike lowered his mouth to her ear. "No running, spitting or shouting by the pool," he teased, his voice low as he held the front door for her.

Clare laughed.

"And," Mrs. Griswold was still harping as they disappeared, "be quiet. The bed and breakfast is full. I don't want to have to call the cops on rowdy behavior...."

They could hear her barking orders even as they reached the car. Pausing, they leaned against the passenger door and, looking at each other with raised eyebrows, burst into laughter.

"How do you propose we get Puddin' past the old battle-ax without getting arrested?" Mike wondered aloud, reaching out and brushing a wispy blond curl away from Clare's eyelashes. He loved the way her eyes sparkled with fun as she gazed up at him.

"I don't know." She giggled, darting a quick glance into the back seat of Mike's car. "Eva would never forgive us if we left him out here. Since he's still out cold, it shouldn't be too hard to smuggle him in. We'll just have to be careful that he doesn't get out and get tanked again," she joked.

Mike laughed. "I'd be only too happy to find us another place to stay, but I'm afraid we got the last two rooms in Happy Valley." He sighed, shifting his weight away from his sore leg. Folding his arms across his chest, he pondered Puddin's playpen and wondered what Mrs. Griswold would make of that particular item. Maybe they should leave it strapped to the roof of his car.

"Oh, I'm sure we'll be fine," Clare said, pulling her princess hat off her head and shaking her hair loose from its bun. "I don't plan on cooking in the room." She laughed. "Or playing loud music."

Mike felt a curious tightening in the pit of his stomach as he watched her finger comb her glorious golden tresses. Did she have any idea at all how stunning she was?

"Where do you stand on the hanky-panky issue?" He smiled rakishly down at her.

Clare turned and, looking over her shoulder at a minxish angle, said, "What? And risk getting thrown out on our ears?"

"It might be worth it," Mike murmured, fighting the urge to grab Clare and give the curmudgeonly Mrs. Griswold an eye full of hanky-panky she wouldn't soon forget. His amorous ambitions surprised him, considering he felt as though he'd single-handedly fought the War of the Roses and lost. Something about the tiny smile that hovered at the corners of her beautiful lips had a way of making him forget the physical discomforts of their dates. Well, almost. Sharp pains radiated up his leg.

With a monumental effort, Mike reined in his galloping libido and began to help Clare unpack the car. Covering Puddin' with his leather jacket, he tucked the still-unconscious mongrel under his arm and, gathering several suitcases, headed with Clare back toward the bed and breakfast.

Inside, Mrs. Griswold was dressing down another couple as they checked in. "No pets, loud noise or cooking in the rooms," she thundered, pointing at them with her bony finger.

Mike looked at Clare in disbelief. "Her rate of return has to be nonexistent," he whispered, wondering how Mrs. Griswold managed to make a go of her business with her attitude problem.

A sharp snort emanated from beneath the leather jacket Mike cradled under his arm as he passed the front desk. "Excuse me," he said politely, and worked his way over to the staircase that led to their rooms.

"Bless you, honey." Clare rushed after him, hoping to avoid Mrs. Griswold's scrutiny, lest the old woman discover them breaking one of her cardinal rules.

Mrs. Griswold drew her thin lips into a tight knot. "Quiet over there." Her voice held an ominous note of warning.

"Wow," Clare breathed as they entered Mike's room and set their belongings, Puddin' included, on his bed. "I didn't expect this at all." Ambling slowly around the delightfully romantic room, Clare decided that the woman behind the front desk had had nothing to do with the decor.

Warm and comfortable, the room gave its guests the feel of coming home. A large Amish four-poster bed sat invitingly in the middle of the room, and was covered with a lovely handcrafted quilt of intricate design. The built-in window seat was covered with bright, fluffy chintz pillows. Above that, several large windows—adorned with yards of gauzy white fabric that billowed in the breeze—overlooked a panoramic view of Happy Valley. Antiques of all shapes and sizes sat in front of walls covered with a cheerful floral wallpaper.

"No kidding," Mike agreed, looking around. "I expected more of a Quonset hut look from old Sarge, down there."

"I wonder if my room looks anything like this." Smiling, she lifted her overnight bag off Mike's bed.

Clare's smile disappeared as she watched him painfully ease himself into an old chair. Poor baby. He'd had such a rough day. Being a knight in shining armor must take a lot out of a guy. She knew it had taken a lot out of her, and she'd been safely out of the way, up in the grandstands.

For a brief moment, back at the jousting tournament, she thought he'd been killed, and had nearly lost her mind with worry. Never before had she ever been quite so fearful as she sat, alternately screaming and praying that he would be all right. She couldn't lose him now. Not when she was beginning to...well...care. Thanking God, she'd cried with relief when he'd finally sat up and waved feebly at the crowd.

She wondered if she should offer to rub his feet. "Are you sure you're okay?"

"Oh, fine. Nothing that a nice, long shower won't cure." He winked at her through lazily hooded eyes. "What do you say we change into something more...comfortable, and then go grab a bite to eat."

Clare felt herself grow warm at his words. "Sounds wonderful. Where should we go?"

Reaching over to the telephone table, Mike picked up the phone and shrugged. "I don't know. Maybe Sarge can tell us." Grinning, he dialed zero and waited. As she heard Mrs. Griswold's gruff greeting from where she stood across the room, Clare's eyes widened nervously. He was even braver than she'd imagined, she thought with admiration. Wasn't he afraid of anything?

"Hi, this is Mike Jacoby in room 5. I was wondering if you had any idea where we could go for dinner." He held the phone away from his ear as Mrs. Griswold shrieked her reply.

"What am I?" Her shrill voice came skidding into the room. *"Some kind of damn travel agent?"* With that, the line went dead.

Mike stared blankly at the receiver for a moment, then shrugged. "I guess we're on our own," he said, grinning as he replaced the receiver in its cradle. He glanced over to the bed at the snoring dog. "I think we can probably leave him here for a while. Let sleeping dogs lie and all that. I'm going to clip his leash to the bedpost, just in case he gets any wild ideas, though." He ran a thoughtful hand over his jaw.

"Good idea," Clare agreed, shifting her suitcase in her hands. "Don't bother getting up. I'll just go change and meet you back here in about twenty minutes."

Right next door, in a room that was almost identical to Mike's, Clare unpacked her luggage and, with a huge, deeply heartfelt sigh of relief, removed her medieval-fair costume. Opting for comfort on this particular outing, she changed into a short denim skirt and a soft pink angora sweater, hoping that Mike didn't have any formal ideas about dinner. She would be comfortable on this date, or know the reason why, she thought, pulling on a pair of tennis shoes over her pink ankle socks. After running a quick brush through her hair and freshening her makeup, she grabbed her room key and headed out into the hallway to find Mike already waiting for her there.

Her breathing became shallow, and her heart leapt erratically at the sight of him. He looked so wonderful. His dark hair, still slightly damp from his shower, contrasted beautifully with the white polo shirt that was stretched handsomely over his powerful build. Thankfully the khaki pants he wore were the perfect complement to the casual style she'd chosen for herself.

"Ready?" he asked, his sexy grin exposing his perfect, shiny white teeth.

"Sure." Her reply was shy as she allowed him to take her hand and lead her toward the stairs.

Together they tiptoed past the front desk, even though the cantankerous old Mrs. Griswold was nowhere to be seen. Once they reached the parking lot, Mike paused and glanced longingly at his car.

"I did some calling around while you were changing, and discovered a little place called the Olde English Pub, not too far from here. I'm told they make terrific fish and chips." He tilted his head toward her and gave her a knowing wink. "I thought we could walk."

Eyes darting up at the cloudless twilight sky, and then down at her tennis-shoe-clad feet, Clare nodded. Why not? Although, just how far was "not too far"? she wondered. Knowing the way Mike liked to walk, they would undoubtedly work off the entire fish-and-chip dinner before the evening was over.

"Sounds delicious," she agreed. Her eyes slid down to his own tennis shoes. "Are you sure you're okay to walk? How is your ankle feeling?"

Mike inhaled sharply and sent her a broad smile. "Just great."

Clare was glad, but had to wonder at the slight hitch in his get-along. Obviously he was experiencing some pain. Oh, well, she wouldn't deprive him of the pleasure of his walk by insisting that they drive, no matter how much she preferred taking the car.

Besides, the spring evening was warm and balmy. They would probably be just fine, she decided. The scent of flowering bushes and fresh-cut grass commingled, giving off a pleasant aroma as they strolled companionably along through the quaint little village of Happy Valley. The sun set amid a riot of breathtaking reds and oranges, and one by one the stars began to sparkle in the darkening sky.

They chatted chummily about anything and everything that happened to pop into their minds, each privately thrilled just to be spending time with the other, doing something simple. No strange musical instruments, no exotic drinks, no outlandish clothing. Why couldn't it be exactly like this all the time? they wondered.

Fortunately for Mike's injured ankle, he'd been right and the restaurant was only a short distance from the bed and breakfast. The charming little Olde English Pub looked like a cottage straight out of a fairy tale. Tables were scattered out-of-doors, in romantic nooks and crannies of the large English garden that surrounded the cottage proper. A string quartet played soft chamber music in the background as the hostess seated Clare and Mike in a secluded area shrouded by several blossoming trees.

Eternally grateful to finally be off his throbbing foot, Mike relaxed and watched Clare over the cheerful flames that danced at the tips of the candles on their table. She was so beautiful in the candlelight. Pensively nibbling her lower lip, she scanned the menu, and he wondered what she could be thinking.

Thank heavens they don't serve piña coladas, Clare thought, and reviewing the beverage listings, decided on iced tea. Closing her menu, she smiled across the table at Mike. "What are you going to have?" she asked.

You, he wanted to say. "Well, the special is crusty bread and turkey legs," he teased, "but since we had that for lunch, I think I'll go for the fish and chips."

Clare laughed. "Me, too." She tossed her menu on top of his. This was so much fun. Mike was so wonderful. Just being with him had her stomach somersaulting with excitement. As far as she was concerned, they never had to go anywhere again, just as long as she could bask in the thrill of his presence. "I'm so glad that you're all right. I was pretty worried about you there during the jousting tournament." He would never know just how worried, she thought.

"To tell you the truth—" Mike's eyes twinkled merrily in the candlelight "—I was, too. Nothing like being clotheslined by a jousting lance."

He stretched, pulling the white fabric of his polo shirt taut across his broad chest, and it was all Clare could do not to stare.

"I'm just glad you're...feeling okay now," she said, and wondered vaguely if he was really as well built as he appeared to be under that shirt of his. Luckily the waitress appeared and diverted her attention by taking their order.

"Yes. I'm feeling much better, thanks." As the waitress moved away with their menus, Mike shrugged. It was true. He did feel wonderful. Thanks due—in no small part—to the fact that he was simply spending time with her. With the exception of his ankle and a slight headache and, well, some bumps and bruises he didn't feel like discussing, he'd never felt better. More alive. More vital. "So, what do you know about the poet who owns the farm where the fair was held today?'' he asked, attempting to make conversation about some of the interests she'd alluded to on the note he'd found in the suit pocket.

Clare looked blankly at him, trying to remember the name of the guy that Lucy had said threw the bizarre medieval bash every year. ''I, uh,'' she stammered and shrugged apologetically, ''I'm sorry. I don't know anything about him.'' Now, ask her which century the close-fitting jupon replaced the medieval surcoat, and she could give him a few details. Why hadn't she thought that he might ask her something about the poet? she silently berated herself. There seemed to be no end to her ignorance. How was she ever going to impress upon someone as sharp as Mike that she actually had a brain in her head?

''I've never heard of him, either,'' Mike admitted, glad that he wasn't alone in his ignorance. ''I just thought you might have run across him at a poetry reading or something. I know you enjoy that type of thing.''

Clare frowned, but before she could wonder too much about where he'd gotten the idea that she was a poetry fan, the waitress arrived with two baskets of piping hot fish and chips. It didn't matter anyway. Not wanting to reveal how really stupid she was on the topic of poets and their works, she changed the subject.

''I love fish and chips,'' she bubbled, pulling her basket in front of her and popping a golden fried potato into her mouth. She hadn't realized how truly hungry she was. Her morning doughnut and the few bites of turkey she'd had at lunch were far from her usual daily requirements.

''Umm. Me, too. With lots of catsup,'' Mike said, loading his basket with half the bottle.

''Oh, yes,'' Clare agreed rapturously. ''And tartar sauce. Can't forget the tartar sauce.'' She grinned happily. Sometimes, if she didn't count the costumes and music and penchant for walking, it seemed as if they had a lot in common.

As they walked down the hallway toward the door to her room at the Happy Valley Bed and Breakfast, Clare decided that she'd never had quite so much fun on a date. She couldn't remember laughing quite so hard or feeling quite so attractive in a man's eyes. Mike Jacoby was one of a kind, she thought as he paused in front of her door and turned to look down at her.

"I had a great time tonight," he said, reaching up and running a hand around the back of her neck under her hair.

"Me, too," she breathed, her eyes seeking and finding his.

This time there was nothing awkward about their goodnight kiss. As though it were the moment they'd both been waiting for all their lives, they came together in an embrace so natural it seemed as if they'd been created specifically to fit each other.

Suddenly Mike's bruised and battered body was literally singing with life. He had feelings, both physical and emotional, that he'd never experienced before with another woman. Gathering her up against the solid wall of his body, he leaned heavily against her door and forgot the pain that throbbed in his ankle, his head . . . his back . . . and instead, gave himself up to the pleasure of Clare's heart-stopping kiss.

Time suspended as they moved together in the darkened passage, neither one wanting the moment to end, but both aware that—unfortunately it had to. Interminable moments passed before, with a ragged breath, Mike pulled back and, grasping Clare firmly by her upper arms, looked deeply into her eyes. Could she tell how much he wanted her? he wondered as he let his forehead rest lightly against hers and tried to pull himself together. His pulse roared in his ears.

"I'm about two seconds away from breaking Sarge's hanky-panky rule," he whispered against her cheek as she nibbled on his earlobe. "However," he moaned as Clare began doing things to his neck that none of his other girlfriends had ever thought of, "I don't...mmm....want us to...mmm...get thrown out on our..." Grabbing Clare's arms, he pinned them against her door above her head, and kissed her long and hard. "You're not making this any easier." His voice was raspy against her lips.

"Sorry." Her breathing sounded as ragged as his own.

Slowly he released her arms and smiled ruefully down at her. Clare was far too special to him to risk losing by prematurely pushing their relationship. There was plenty of time for that later, when they knew each other better. However, at the rate he was beginning to care for her, it wouldn't be long. If he didn't know better, he'd almost think he was falling in love with her. Shaking his head to clear it of this insane school of thought, he took a step back. How could he be in love with a woman who had such nutty ideas about dating? He must have taken a much heavier blow to the head than he'd originally thought.

As she smiled that fetching smile that turned his insides to mush, Clare retrieved her room key from her pocket and said, "Thank you for an interesting day. I had a great time." Her brow furrowed slightly. "Will you be okay with Puddin'?"

"Yeah," Mike said stupidly, thinking how unfair it was that he would be spending the night in his romantic little room with the disgusting dog.

"Well," she whispered, her voice sexy and low, "I'll see you in the morning."

"Yeah," Mike said again, and watched her disappear into her room. Shuffling dazedly to his door, he searched his pants pockets for the key to his room. Hmm. Odd. What could he have done with his key? It was then, as he stood alone in the silent and empty hallway, that he realized he'd left the key sitting on his nightstand.

He glanced at his watch. After nine. Damn. Plowing his hands through his hair, he stood there for a moment, attempting to gather his wits. Looking up and down the hallway, he wondered what he should do. There didn't seem to be any way to get into the room, unless he could somehow manage to squeeze through the glass window above his door. Unfortunately, at well over six feet tall, it would probably be easier to get the proverbial camel through an eye of a needle. Maybe Clare would have an idea, he thought and, grateful for an excuse to see her again, moved back toward her room.

"Clare?" He tapped lightly on her door. He could hear her rustling around inside.

"Yes?"

She cracked her door open, and he could see that she'd changed into a skimpy pair of baby-doll pajamas. His Adam's apple collided with his collar. Wow. She was spectacular. The itty-bitty silky-looking sleepwear hung artlessly on her athletic build, and had him dying to reach out and see if her skin was really as smooth and firm as it looked in the golden light of her lamp.

"I, uh, don't have my key."

The door swung wide. "You're kidding."

"Well, no. I think I left it on my nightstand. And unfortunately, it's after nine o'clock. I'm afraid we can't ask Sarge to let me in."

Clare grinned. "No. Not unless you want her to hand you your head on a platter."

Mike returned her grin. "No, thanks. One mortal blow to the head a day is enough for this guy."

Together they walked out into the hallway and stood in front of Mike's door and wondered in hushed voices how they could get inside.

"I know you might find this hard to believe," Clare said, looking playfully up at Mike, "but Puddin' can do a few tricks. Eva taught him to fetch once. Maybe I could talk to him through the window above your door." She tilted her head back and considered the prospect. "I'll tell him to set the key on a piece of newspaper that we'll slide under the door."

Mike ran a thoughtful hand over the stubble on his jaw. "Worth a try," he whispered skeptically. The dog was worthless stone-cold sober, let alone with a hangover. But he was willing to do anything to get off his aching ankle.

Tiptoeing quickly to her room, Clare searched for a newspaper, but could only find a sheet of notebook paper. It was small, but it would have to do. She wondered briefly if she should change into something a little less revealing, but deciding there wasn't time, hurried back out to the hall to join Mike. After sliding the paper halfway under his door, she turned to face him.

"Do you feel well enough to give me a boost up to the window?" she asked worriedly. After the fall he'd taken today, she was surprised he was even still standing. But it was their only hope. As big as he was, it would be out of the question for her to lift him.

His eyes dropped to her fetching lingerie, and he swallowed. Oh, brother. Between her hard body and his contusions and abrasions, he was going to keel over for sure.

"You bet," he asserted manfully. No problem. Piece of cake. She could always take him to the emergency room later. Moving around behind her, he placed his hands around her slender waist. He bit back a groan of frustration. Oh, man, she was even firmer than she looked. "On the count of three," he whispered.

"Okay," she nodded, and counted aloud with him. "One... twooo... huuff... threeeee!" And suddenly she found herself airborne, struggling to find a purchase for her feet somewhere in the vicinity of his broad shoulders. "Sorry." She giggled and wildly circled her arms as she fought for balance. "I didn't mean to tear your ears off there," she gasped, and clutched the top of the doorframe for balance. Heavens. He'd lifted her as easily as he would a feather pillow, she thought, marveling at how strong he was. Especially considering how tall she was. And even though she worked hard to stay in shape, she knew it took a powerful man to lift her this way.

"No sweat," he rasped, staggering under his load, sure that his ankle had finally laid down and died. He gripped her calves to steady her, and tried to focus on the supple, smooth muscles that strained beneath his fingers. She really did have great legs. Too bad he wasn't in any position to enjoy them.

"Try to stand still," Clare panted, stretching toward the window to get a better view of the dog. "Too bad you didn't leave your light on," she lamented. "It's dark in there."

"Sorry," Mike grunted, fishing one of her toes out of his ear. "Next time I'll try to remember that."

"Here, Puddin'," she whispered, and tapped on the window. "Come on, puppy. Come to Auntie Clare."

Puddin's bark sounded decidedly disoriented.

"Shh, Puddin'," she warned. "Don't speak."

"Woooff!" Puddin' barked. "Errrrr... Wooooooffffff! Wooooooffffff!"

"Is he coming?" Mike's muscles shrieked in agony.

"I'm not sure. My eyes are adjusting to the darkness," she mumbled, and pressed her nose to the glass and shielded her eyes against the hall light with her hands. "Uh-oh . . ."

"What, uh-oh?" Mike huffed, sliding his hands up her shapely thighs, partly for balance and partly to take his mind off the agony that radiated from his leg. She really had great thighs. So firm. So nicely muscled.

"I think I remember you tying him to the bed."

Now she remembers, he thought grumpily.

"And," she continued, still peering into his room, "if he's clipped to the bed, he won't be able to bring the ke—"

Mike felt her legs go rigid beneath his hands.

"Oh, no!" she gasped, panic filling her voice.

"What, oh no?"

"Someone's coming!"

Her feet rocked back and forth on his shoulders in an incredibly painful manner, and for just a second he was afraid they were going to collapse and land in a heap on the floor. Sure enough, an elderly-looking woman was emerging from her room at the end of the hall and heading toward them. Probably on her way to the communal bathroom, he thought, noting her towel and toothbrush as Clare lifted her foot away from his eyes.

"Don't panic," he ordered up at her from between his clenched teeth. He pushed her delectable bottom off his head and back up where it belonged. "Just play it cool."

"Oh, sure. Cool. Just hangin' in the hallway. Like normal," she muttered, swaying crazily. "I just know she heard the dog. She's probably going downstairs right now to complain. We're in big trouble now," she moaned, then smiled at the woman's approach.

"Hi," Clare said blithely.

"Hi," the woman answered, slowing at her approach and adjusting her spectacles, then eyed them with a befuddled expression on her face.

Noting her curiosity, Clare explained for the woman's benefit. "Puddin' hates to be left alone." She shrugged sheepishly.

The gray-haired woman smiled broadly. "My husband is the same way," she said, and disappeared into the bathroom.

"What did she say?" Clare grunted as Mike lifted her off his shoulders and set her on the ground.

"Beats me." He shrugged and rotated his neck and shoulders, just to make sure they were still connecting his head to his body.

"What now?" she asked, wishing she didn't feel quite so naked, standing out there in the hallway in her baby-dolls.

"I could sleep in the tub, if Grandma there—" he gestured toward the bathroom "—wouldn't mind."

Clare giggled. "Oh, yeah. I'm sure the guests would love having you snoring away in the tub while they do their business." Slipping her hand into the crook of his arm, she tugged him into her room and shut the door. They were obviously out of options. He would have to stay in here with her tonight. The shape he was in, she had little fear that they would be breaking Mrs. Griswold's hanky-panky rule. "You can have the bed," she said magnanimously, gesturing to the Amish four-poster as she turned to face him. "I'll take the window seat."

"Clare, I'm not kicking you out of your bed," he argued, suddenly so exhausted he could hardly think straight. "I'll sleep on the floor."

"Don't be ridiculous," she cried. "You're in no shape to sleep on the floor."

He had to agree. She was right. He wasn't even in any shape to sleep on the bed. "Well, okay. We could share if you want to." Sinking to the edge of the bed, he drew his ankle up over his knee and probed the swollen joint with his fingertips. "I can guarantee that your virtue would be safe with me, tonight anyway."

Her heart went out to him as he winced in pain. "Maybe you should see a doctor," she suggested.

"Nah. I'll be okay. I just need to... lay down for a minute." Flopping back on the bed, he moaned.

"I think I have some aspirin in my purse," she volunteered.

"Mmm. That's a good idea." He opened an eye and nodded weakly. "Bring the whole bottle."

Clare grabbed her purse and rooted around inside till she came up with the painkillers. Perching on the bed beside him, she handed him the bottle and pulled the quilt up over him. "Here you go. Why don't you sleep here, and I'll lay the opposite direction by the headboard? Sarge shouldn't have any objection to that," she said.

Mike grinned and then lay perfectly still. "Do you hear that?"

"What?"

"Listen."

Strains of Puddin's midnight, post-party escapades reached them through the wall between their rooms. Muffled howling, accompanied by wheezing, hacking, snorting and several loud, unidentifiable thumps reached their ears.

Mike sat up and leaned with Clare toward the wall.

"Do you think he's okay?" Clare asked, wondering at what moment Sarge would burst through the door, guns blazing.

"I don't know," Mike said doubtfully.

They listened with growing apprehension as Puddin's howls reached a crescendo.

"It sounds like he's trying to bust out of jail," Clare said, referring to the repetitive thumping. There was a loud crash, and then . . . silence. They sat listening carefully for a while longer. "I guess he's . . . done."

She shrugged and smiled shyly at Mike. It seemed so strange to have him sitting there at the end of her bed. Awkward, but certainly not unpleasant. No, even though he looked like death warmed over, it would be fun knowing that as she lay dreaming of him, he was no more than an arm's length away.

Mike flopped back on the bed. "He'll be fine," he assured Clare. At least the obnoxious animal would be fine till he got a hold of him, he thought grimly, and shook a handful of aspirin into his palm. He swallowed them without benefit of water, grimacing as they ground their way down his throat.

Clare turned out the light and crawled into bed alongside the headboard. She lay, listening to him breathe, and wondered how she would ever get a wink of sleep. Her thoughts drifted back over the day, and once again she was amazed at how much closer she felt to Mike—even after such a short time—than she ever had to Beau.

She just couldn't puzzle it out. Why? *Why* was she so comfortable with him? He was so different, in so many fundamental ways. Perhaps she was just one of those women who always chose the completely wrong man. Just like Eva. Sighing, she burrowed under her blankets as well as she could, considering Mike pinned most of them under his body at the end of the bed, and snuggled into her pillow.

"Clare?"

His whisper sounded so close in the pitch blackness of their room.

"Hmm?"

"I just wanted you to know that I didn't forget my key on purpose."

Smiling into the darkness, she said, "Oh, I know." And she did. That was just one of the wonderful, gentlemanly things about Mike Jacoby that she loved.

8

"Good morning," Clare whispered, and smiled self-consciously at Mike. Lying propped on an elbow at the end of her bed, he had obviously been watching her sleep. Good heavens, she thought, pushing her tangled blond mop away from her eyes, she must look perfectly dreadful. But then, what else was new? Dates with Mike had a way of destroying every effort she made in the beauty department.

"Good morning," he whispered back.

"Why are we whispering?"

"Well," he said, stretching and yawning appealingly, then, rolling onto his stomach, grinned at her, "I don't know about you, but I'm afraid of what will happen if Mrs. Griswold finds out we broke two of her house rules."

Giggling, Clare sat up and tucked her legs under her body. "Well, at least we didn't cook in the room."

Mike arched a roguish eyebrow. "Not because I wasn't tempted."

She cast her eyes down at the blanket that lay across her lap and plucked bashfully at the fuzzy threads she found there. Peeking up at him from the wispy curtain of her bangs, she asked, "How do you suppose we should go about getting into your room?"

He thoughtfully scratched the whiskers that shadowed his cheeks and chin. "I've been giving that some thought. I think I'll go downstairs, damn the torpedoes and tell Mrs. Griswold I locked myself out. Hopefully she'll just give me a key and won't insist on letting me back into the room herself. And if we're really lucky, she'll have slept through the racket the mutt made last night.''

"Are you feeling lucky?" Clare asked teasingly.

Mike looked at her for a long, unreadable moment, then a slow, sexy grin tipped the corners of his mouth. "Yes," he whispered, "I'm feeling incredibly lucky."

As luck would have it, they were lucky. Mrs. Griswold had given Mike a key with an impatient frown, and didn't mention hearing any kind of unusual noise coming from his room last night. And Puddin'—though it had sounded as if he'd torn the place apart the night before—had done nothing more than chew one of Mike's antlers off his medieval headdress.

All in all, things worked out pretty well, Mike thought with relief as he sat across from Clare at the breakfast table. Even his leg was feeling a hundred percent better this morning. And waking up with Clare? Well, that made the entire weekend worthwhile. The speeding ticket, being knocked senseless by a jousting lance, the less than friendly Mrs. Griswold . . . all of it had been tolerable and even fun because of the lovely lady that sat smiling at him.

He watched with interest the way her lips caressed the rim of her coffee cup as she allowed her eyes to travel around the room. She stopped and stared, and Mike followed her gaze to see what she was looking at.

"What's wrong?" he asked, reaching out and lacing his fingers with hers.

"Oh—" She gave her head a light shake and nibbled the small smile at her lips. "Nothing, really. The lady who passed us in the hall last night just came into the room with her husband.''

"Oh." He nodded. "And they're coming this way."

As the elderly woman and her husband made their way past their table, they paused.

"Are you all right, deary? We heard all the racket last night, and just wondered if you were feeling okay. All that moaning and thumping, gracious sakes!" the woman exclaimed.

"I'm fine," Clare assured her. "Puddin' gets kind of crazy when he's tied up for long."

"Oh?" The old woman arched an inquisitive brow. She glanced warily at Mike.

"Yes," Clare continued. "I'm sorry if he disturbed you. It's just that he wanted his mommy. Usually he'll wear himself out crying, and then fall asleep. That's why I don't spank him."

The woman exchanged glances with her husband, and moved off to her table. Her husband paused next to Mike.

"Saw you at the jousting tournament yesterday. Take my advice and stick with the indoor sports." He chuckled and followed his wife.

Clare frowned at Mike. "What's that supposed to mean?"

"Beats me."

The following Monday, Sam, Bart and Roger sat at the break table, inside the garage at Seattle Import Repair.

"How'd it go?" Bart asked as Mike grabbed a folding metal chair and, stuffing it between his legs, dropped into the seat and dangled his elbows over the backrest.

"You're fired," he snapped testily, and rubbed the still black-and-blue areas behind his neck and shoulders.

Bart laughed. "Another bad one, huh?"

"Yup," Mike sighed, and much to the cackling and hooting delight of his employees, regaled them with tales of his brief stint as a knight in shining armor over the weekend.

"Yeah," Bart chuckled, "the kids said they saw you lyin' on your can out there in the middle of the field. I guess you were one of the highlights of the whole deal. Hell, they're still talkin' about how you looked like that guy on TV—you know the one—the agony of defeat?"

Sam winced. "Ouch."

"I'm so glad I could help entertain the troops," Mike said, his voice dripping with sarcasm. "Man, Bart, nothing against your kids, but those medieval-fair people are really strange."

Bart laughed, taking no offense. "I know. The kids say that's the main reason they go."

"So, what's next?" Sam wanted to know.

"No more medieval fairs, I can tell you that much," Mike sighed, and fished his wallet out of his back pocket. Pulling the much studied and slightly tattered note from Clare out of the leather billfold and smoothing it on the tabletop, he glanced around the table at his three curious friends and winced. "Looks like Modern poetry."

Roger blew a series of cigar smoke rings at the ceiling and, frowning reflectively, tapped his ashes on the concrete floor. "My wife likes that kind of junk, too." Angling his grisly head at Mike, he chewed the damp, sticky tip of his stogie. "She's got season tickets to some kind of uppity gig that the Modern Poets' Society puts on every Friday night. We're leaving town this weekend. She won't be able to use 'em. Why don't I bring 'em in for you and Clare?"

Reaching for the phone, Mike rolled his eyes. "Okay, why not. First, though, I'll see if she can make it."

"Wow," Sam commented. "You really must like this woman. Do you think maybe she's the one?"

Mike paused, and all three men leaned forward to listen. "Yeah," he exhaled noisily, and shook his head. "After all, why let a little thing like . . . nothing in common stop us?" Grinning at the ribald laughter that rippled around the table, he picked up the phone and dialed Monaco's men's department.

Clare's mortified gaze traveled around the highly fashionable crowd that stood in the elegant old lobby of the Performing Arts Theater in downtown Seattle. Everyone, it seemed, was dressed to the nines. Diamonds, furs, sequins . . . and that was just the ushers. What had Mike been thinking when he'd advised her to dress casually? Hopelessly out of place in her ski jacket and loose-fit blue jeans, she couldn't have been more conspicuous if she'd shown up naked. Her only consolation, she thought, looking over at Mike's glum profile, was that she wasn't the only one. No, together they looked like a couple of ski-bum party crashers.

Normally, Clare mused—as she prayed she wouldn't run into anyone she knew—she would be wringing Mike's neck for the bum steer in the attire department. But she was too busy being grateful that this particular event didn't require a costume.

Besides, tuxedo or no, Mike Jacoby was definitely the best-looking man there. He's just not a slave to fashion, she thought, once more giving him the benefit of the doubt. But she had to wonder about his love for Modern poetry. He seemed more the *Sports Illustrated* swimsuit-edition type when it came to literature.

The lobby lights dimmed twice, and the chic, tastefully dressed crowd began to throng toward their seats. Oh, well, she decided as Mike took her by the hand and pulled her into the opulent auditorium, she would try to keep an open mind. Do her best to discover what he found so interesting about Modern poetry. At least he wasn't into skydiving, like Beau.

As they settled in next to a snobbish couple that reminded Mike of Lovey and Thurston Howell III from "Gilligan's Island," he helped Clare off with her ski jacket and pointedly ignored Lovey's pained expression. They had just as much right to be there as anyone else.

Although, he thought, mentally chastising himself, just because he figured Roger was a casual kind of guy, he shouldn't have taken it for granted that his wife was, too. Thank heavens Clare hadn't jumped down his throat about the fact that they were the only two people in the entire room not dressed formally. He'd thought he'd been doing her a favor. Tennis shoes had just sounded like such a good idea at the time.

He glanced over at her as she studied the program. She probably already knew about this stuff, he thought, and began looking over his own copy.

Clare studied the program, hoping to glean some kind of information about tonight's proceedings. When it came to Modern poetry—as with everything else Mike was interested in—she was clueless. What on earth could she say, she wondered, that could impress him? Her knowledge of the subject was limited, to say the least.

Mike dropped a casual hand on her knee, and Clare glanced up at him. He winked possessively at her, and she could feel the warmth radiate up her leg and into her heart. Somehow the simple gesture made the fact that they were completely underdressed suddenly unimportant.

"I like a good poem," she said brightly, hoping to get the conversational ball rolling.

"Me, too," Mike said tentatively. "I'm partial to limericks." Lovey turned and scowled at him. "Those ones about the guy from Nantucket never fail to crack me up." Lovey snorted in disgust.

Clare nodded, having no idea what he meant or why the snob sitting next to Mike kept giving them dirty looks. "I've always enjoyed Bob Dylan's work," she said assertively. Or was it Dylan Thomas? She always got those two confused....

After some more inane, idle chitchat, the auditorium finally—and thankfully—darkened. A spotlight flashed on, illuminating a lone woman, standing in the middle of the stage dressed in military fatigues.

The fashionably togged audience went wild.

Clare and Mike clapped enthusiastically and, smiling broadly at each other, wondered what all the fuss was about. A hush fell over the room, and the woman on the stage glared out at the audience, remaining silent for so long, Clare began to fidget nervously. Had she forgotten her lines?

Apparently not, she decided, as the woman finally spoke.

"Many women store hatred in their hips," she cried.

The crowd went wild. Figuring, why not? Clare applauded and nodded pleasantly at Mike. He was so Continental, she thought, watching him bring his strong, well-formed hands together in appreciation of the art he obviously thought so highly of.

"And," the woman continued, "anger...in their thighs." The poet paused, and Clare began to clap, until she realized she was the only one. Embarrassed, she glanced sheepishly at Mike. How could he tell when it was time to applaud? she wondered, embarrassed. It was clear he'd been around the poetry block a time or two.

"My thighs are angry!" the poet shouted.

"Angry!"

The crowd applauded.

"Angry!"

Clare applauded. The crowd remained silent.

This was harder to get the hang of than advanced bench aerobics, she fumed. She was beginning to get a little angry herself. Perhaps this was why it seemed her thighs were beginning to heat up. But then again, that could have something to do with Mike's hand resting lightly on her leg, just above her knee.

"War!" the militant poet shouted. "What is it good for?"

Absolutely nothin'! Yes! Clare thought triumphantly. Finally a bit of poetry she recognized. However, relieved as she was, she kept her hands firmly locked in her lap.

Colored lights began to swirl around the stage, and strobes flashed until both Clare and Mike began to fear for their eyesight. Bizarre celestial music reached a frenzied pitch as the militant poet was joined on the stage by other similarly dressed poets.

"War!" they shouted. "War! Pillage...the...village."

Clare frowned. What on earth could this mean?

"Pillage...the...village," they chanted over and over, then the strange music came to a grinding halt, and once more silence reigned.

"Is it any wonder that my thighs are angry?" the original militant poet asked in a small voice.

The lights flashed off, and once again the crowd went wild. Clare glanced at Mike. Would she ever really understand what made him tick?

Next the militant poet was replaced by a man, dressed in blue street clothes, who sat in a large, overstuffed bright blue chair at the edge of the stage, near the orchestra pit. A dim blue shaft of light bathed him in its eerie glow. Clare shivered, even though the room was growing warm. Very warm, actually. It almost seemed that the audience was breathing up all the air. Mike squeezed her knee, and she looked gratefully up at him. Thank heavens he was here, she thought. He was the one bright spot in this horrific event.

"Blue," the blue poet began reflectively. "Singing the blues...Feeling blue...Blue sky...My blue heaven. My world is...blue. The wind...blew...."

Puzzled, Clare drew her brow together in consternation. Obviously this was all over her head.

"Bluuuuuue," the poet droned on, boring her nearly to tears after the first hour. Stifling a yawn, she leaned drowsily against Mike's strong, comfortable shoulder. Mmm. Yes, she could sit through a reading of the greater-Seattle-area phone book if it meant she could lean on Mike. She smiled contentedly as she felt his head drop onto hers. He smelled so good, she thought, tuning out the rhapsody in blue and tuning into Mike's after-shave. She nuzzled closer into his neck, and closed her eyes. All the better to smell him...my...dear.

Mike would have lost his mind from sheer boredom, if it wasn't for Clare's delightful little nose, which was at the moment buried in his neck. Oh, the things this woman did to his neck. Shivers of delight ran down his spine, which was odd, considering the room was growing hotter than a damn firecracker. He tugged at his collar.

"Blue hair... Bluuuuue balloooooons..." the poet droned on. And on.

What the hell was it with all this blue stuff? Mike wondered irritably. Clare's breath tickled his ear, and he forgot his worries. Her hair smelled so wonderful, he thought, nuzzling the soft locks at the top of her head. Mmm. He could sit here, just like this, for hours, if it meant smelling...her...hair....

Thunderous applause jolted Clare and Mike fully awake. And both of them—not wanting the other to discover that they had accidentally dozed off—clapped and smiled and nodded, as though there were no tomorrow.

Later that evening, as they sat in a casual little pie shop, Clare was finally able to unwind over a cup of coffee. Although, the disconcerting images from the Modern-poetry reading had left an unsettling taste in her mouth.

She had always been very literal in her approach to life, not bothering to look for the deeper meaning or subtext when it came to arts and entertainment. Taking her entertainment at face value, she preferred a good sitcom to an avant-garde, off-Broadway play. And when it came to the fine arts, give her a realistic bowl of fruit over a bunch of squiggly dots and blobs, any day.

Call her a boring homebody, but that's who—it was becoming increasingly clear—she was. Could two people who were obviously worlds apart when it came to this basic view of life ever really be compatible? she wondered, looking across the tabletop over to the shiny red booth where Mike struggled out of his ski jacket. Was it true that opposites attracted? Or did they just eventually end up driving each other crazy with their intrinsic differences?

As Mike pulled several napkins out of the silver dispenser on the tabletop, she tried to envision herself married to him, years down the road. They would have a big family. The one she'd always wanted growing up. Beautiful children that looked just like Mike. They would have a big old house, complete with a picket fence and a dog. And someday, when they were old, they would sit on the front porch and tell their grandchildren about the time grandpa lost the jousting tournament. Clare smiled at the appealing images of herself as Mrs. Mike Jacoby. In some respects, it felt so right. Perfect.

And in other respects, it was horrifying. Would she have to spend the rest of her life gritting her teeth through one increasingly wretched social affair after another? The idea of spending her old age sitting through endless hours of Mike's peculiar side interests struck terror into her heart.

Mike lifted the corners of his sensual mouth, causing the hidden dimples in his cheeks to appear, and it was then, as her pulse reacted, she knew that she was going to have to make some decisions concerning her relationship with him. Probably the hardest decisions she'd ever had to make in her life. For as much as she was drawn to him on many wonderful levels, she was daunted by so many others.

A sudden, overwhelming feeling of sadness stole into her heart. She couldn't face the fact that she might have to give up this man who was coming to mean more to her than anyone had ever meant to her before. How could she have let this happen? How could she have allowed herself to begin falling in love with someone so amazingly different than herself? She knew that the deeper she allowed her life to become entangled with Mike's, the harder it would be when it came time to say goodbye. And they would say goodbye. Sooner or later.

Because when Mike found out the truth...when he found out how much she disliked nearly every social occasion he'd invited her to...when he found out how she'd only been pretending to enjoy his interests...he would be hurt.

The very idea of hurting Mike nearly broke Clare's already fragile heart.

"Gee..." Mike grinned and rolled his napkin into a tight little tube, then proceeded to tear it to shreds. "How about that militant poet, huh?"

Shifting in her seat, Clare forced herself to forget her morose daydreams and concentrate on the joy of the here and now. She may not have any great future with Mike, but at least, for now anyway, she was living on the edge.

"My goodness, yes. Boy, oh boy," she said, hoping she sounded knowledgeable, and above all hoping he didn't realize that she'd slept through the better part of the evening. He'd probably spent a fortune on the tickets. "She was pretty angry. Angry about war. And, of course, her, uh, thighs, and, uh, hips."

The waitress arrived and refilled their cups of coffee.

"Yeah," was all Mike could think of by way of response. She'd probably never forgive him if she knew he'd fallen asleep. "I really thought that the blue poet was, uh, interesting." He could only pray that he hadn't snored while little boy blue was performing.

"Oh, uh-huh. Blue is my favorite color," Clare said.

"Really?" He hadn't known that. But it made perfect sense. Her eyes were the most beautiful sky blue he'd ever seen. She looked great in blue, too. Of course, Clare looked great in just about anything, he mused, thinking back to her fetching medieval costume.

Deciding to steer the topic to safer ground, Mike said, "You know, if the alterations are done on my suit, I should probably come in to the store this week and pick it up."

Clare brightened. "Oh, yes. They've been done for a couple days now. I've been meaning to tell you, but…we've been so busy."

"That's great. My sister will be glad. Mom's big surprise birthday bash is next week. She'll be sixty. I can hardly believe it. She still looks and acts like a kid."

"Next week? Really? My birthday is the week after that."

"No kidding. What day?"

"April 2."

"Hey, well, we'll have to do something to celebrate," Mike suggested enthusiastically.

Clare stiffened, hoping her smile was convincing. "That would be great." Just what did he have in mind? An evening with an Elvis impersonator? A Bigfoot-hunting expedition? Flame throwing?

Again Mike smiled, and again Clare forgot her troubles. Whatever he had in mind, she would cross that bridge when she came to it. In the meantime, she was just going to enjoy these few precious moments of normalcy sitting in a booth at the pie shop with Mike. And she would try not to think about the future.

Mike sat in his car and tried to bring his erratic breathing under control before he attempted to drive himself home from Clare's place. When it came to Clare, there should be a law. Don't kiss and drive. Her kisses were far headier than all the piña coladas they'd drunk on their first date, combined.

Pulling his keys out of his pocket and squeezing them tightly in his hand, Mike willed his blood pressure to lower to a less dangerous level. Man, how he wanted her. From the moment he'd first laid eyes on her, she'd become a constant, insatiable craving, driving him slowly out of his mind. He couldn't seem to get enough of her. The smell of her perfume, the feel of her hands in his hair, the taste of her sweet kiss. Sighing raggedly, he ran a shaky hand across his jaw.

She had gone inside ages ago, and he was still reeling from the effects of her mind-drugging good-night kisses. She was probably already in bed by now, he thought, and then groaned aloud as he remembered waking up in her bed and the silky smoothness of her long, supple, athletic legs and the skimpy baby-dolls she wore over them.

Never before had any woman felt so right in his arms. Responded to him the way she did. She was sexy, smart, even-tempered and beautiful. Everything he'd ever wanted in a woman.

He was going to lose his mind.

Would he ever be able to get her out of his system? More than anything, he wanted to bring their relationship to a more intimate level. To commit to her. To be with her always.

To ask her to marry him.

But how the hell could he do that when he couldn't stand any of her nutty, funky ideas about spending free time? Maybe, he thought as an idea began to form in his head, just maybe they should try things his way for a change. Couldn't hurt to try, he decided, roughly shoving his key into the ignition. No, it certainly couldn't hurt to try.

9

---•---

"*A cruise?*" Mike tucked his pencil behind his ear and stared blankly at his sister. Priscilla wanted to get their mother a cruise for her birthday? He'd been thinking of something more along the lines of say...a scarf. But, he knew as he watched Priss tap her foot impatiently—anxious to get out of the garage and back to her job—it would be easier not to argue. One way or another, Priss always got what she wanted.

"Yes, a *cruise,*" Priscilla said snippily, as though she were stating the obvious. "Ryan, Barry and Landon have already given me their checks. *They* thought it was a great idea."

Of course they did, he thought irritably. His three older brothers knew it was no use arguing with their headstrong sister. Sighing, he grabbed his checkbook out of his desk and, writing the stated amount on a blank check, tossed it at Priscilla. "Here," he said resignedly, "have fun."

"Thanks, Mikey. You're a love," she chirped breezily, and slipped his check into her purse. Turning to leave his office, which was situated behind the garage's lube bay, she paused and looked over her shoulder on her way out the door. "I have to get going. Now that I have your go-ahead on the cruise, everything's all set for Saturday night."

"Glad I could be of assistance," Mike said dryly. He pushed himself away from his desk and, standing, walked her toward her car.

"Your suit is back from the tailor's?" It was a rhetorical question. Priss had a way of nagging without really seeming like she was nagging.

Shaking his head, Mike glanced up at the ceiling. "Yes, and I'm going to go pick it up this afternoon. Which reminds me," he said as he opened her car door for her, "I'd like to bring a date to Mom's birthday."

Priscilla stopped dead in her tracks and, turning sharply, looked up at him with interest. "Anyone I know?"

"No. But she's..."

"What?"

"Special. She's very special. And I'm kind of worried that she might not have a good time. A party at the country club isn't really her kind of thing."

Arching a delicate brow, Priscilla said, "Oh? And what, pray tell, is her kind of... *thing?* Mikey, she's not underage, is she?" She looked positively horrified.

Mike shook his head. *Oh, no, no, no.* He wasn't going to let Priss in on what he'd been going through lately for Clare. She would laugh herself sick. "It's a long story. Just tell me if I can bring a date or not."

Priscilla dropped into the front seat of her car. "Sure. I don't care. I'm bringing one myself." She started her engine and adjusted her rearview mirror.

Never able to resist giving the boss's stuck-up sister a bad time about her driving, Bart, Roger and Sam all dived for cover.

"Very funny," she called drolly, and with a little wave at her younger brother, drove away.

"So," Sam grunted, climbing out of the lube bay, "we couldn't help but overhear that you're bringing Clare to your mom's party."

"Time to meet the family, huh?" Bart elbowed Roger.

"Yeah." Mike shrugged as he followed the three men over to the break table. Taking a seat with them, he said, "I just hope she has a good time. According to the note, she likes wild parties. The country club isn't exactly wild."

"Unless you're already dead." Sam nodded in agreement.

Mike leaned back on the hind legs of his chair and glanced around the table at the three men who worked for him. "You know, I've been thinking, Clare's birthday is the week after Mom's. Maybe I should throw her a surprise party. A big, hairy, wild party that she'll never forget. Then I will have met every requirement on her note. I'll be—" he grinned cockily "—her dream man."

Bart lifted and dropped his shoulders. "Who knows. Maybe a party would cinch the deal. My kids have some friends who are in a band. You know, one of those screaming, long-haired, tattooed, brain-fried, every-father's-nightmare kind of bands. They work cheap."

Sam nodded thoughtfully. "We could have the party here, at the garage. Since it's such a big place, we could make a lot of noise, and no neighbors would complain. And we could also invite a lot of people that way."

Suddenly swept up in the excitement of the idea, Mike grabbed a pad and the pencil from behind his ear, and began making notes. "Okay, Bart, you're in charge of the music. Sam, you're in charge of the decorations. You can help me make a guest list, too." Sam nodded happily and Mike turned to Roger. "Rog, old man, what can you do?"

Roger thought for a moment. "My wife and a bunch of ladies from her social circle threw a party for some gal from

the Modern Poets' Society. They all agreed the highlight of
the evening was this team of Chippendale-type dancers that
came to entertain them.''

"I don't know," Mike said dubiously. Then he shrugged.
Ah, what the heck. It was her birthday. If she wanted wild,
he'd give her the wildest. Nodding at Roger, he said, "Go
for it."

Up, up and away-ee-yea. Mike hummed along under his
breath with the piped-in music as he threaded his way back
to the men's department at Monaco's. *In my beautiful,
my...* He spotted Clare helping a customer. "Beautiful..." he murmured. He could swear that she just got
prettier every time he saw her.

As she glanced up from the couple she was helping, she
caught his eye, and he felt his blood run hot. Oh, man. He
was in deep. Way, way, way over his head with this woman.
But for some reason, the thought of becoming so completely involved with Clare didn't bother him. Not the way
it had with Shawna or Joanne.

Would ya like to fly... in my beautiful, my beautiful...
Mike wandered aimlessly for a while until finally, after what
seemed like a lifetime, Clare was free.

"Hi."

"Hi, yourself." She hated the juvenile way she blushed
every time he smiled at her with that laid-back, boyish
charm of his. What was he doing here? She wished she'd
known he was coming; she would have fussed with her hair
and lipstick.

"I just stopped by to pick up my suit. Mom's party is this
weekend."

"Oh, of course," she said, smiling. She'd known that. It
was just so hard to think straight when he stood so close that
way. And looked at her with a hunger that mirrored her

own. Crooking her finger for him to follow, she led him toward the rack at the back of the department where the recently altered suits were hung. Handing the plastic garment bag to him, she said, "I hope it fits. Maybe you should try it on before the party, just to be sure."

Mike was watching her so closely, she suddenly felt flustered.

"Sure," he said, casually slinging the suit over his shoulder. Then, leaning against the wall, he crossed his ankles and paused, seeming to search for the right words.

Her heart pounded fearsomely. Whatever he was going to say, it looked pretty serious. *Please don't let it be another country fair,* she silently pleaded.

"Clare, I know that this isn't the kind of thing you're usually up for, but I was wondering if you'd consider being my guest at my mother's birthday party this Saturday night. It's going to be kind of a low-key affair, just a few close friends and family, out at the country club. If it doesn't sound too dull, I'd love it if you could come."

Clare's spirits soared and her heart sang. A regular date? At the country club? A low-key affair with just a few close friends and family? Had she died and gone to heaven? Giddy at the prospect, she had to force herself not to jump up and down with joy.

"I'd love that," she said, her voice so cool and sophisticated, it surprised even herself.

"Great." He looked relieved. "Why don't I pick you up at your place, say around six-thirty?"

"I'll be ready," she promised, shivering at the exciting prospect of a normal date with the man she was very much afraid she was beginning to love.

At long last, Saturday had arrived, and Clare, nervous as a teenager on her first date, arranged her hair into the dozenth hairstyle of the evening. Hurriedly spritzing her chic, upswept chignon one last time for good measure, she tossed the hair-spray bottle into her bathroom sink and, checking her periwinkle blue strapless cocktail dress in the mirror, ran to answer the insistently ringing doorbell.

As she pulled open her front door, she found a very agitated, nearly panic-stricken Mike, wearing the double breasted charcoal gray wool suit that—at one time—had fit him like a glove. Pushing past her and into her living room, he tore at his hair with agitated hands.

"What the hell is wrong with this suit?" he cried, gesturing at the ill-fitting garment that lay spasmodically on his large frame, bunching and hunching, too short here and too long there.

Flabbergasted, Clare stared at the pant legs, which now seemed to be two different lengths altogether, both, of course, wrong. The buttons, no longer in tidy rows, were nowhere near the buttonholes, and the collar... What in heaven's name had Henri done to the collar? Clare wondered, biting back a wave of hysteria. Only Elvis could pull that look off, and even that was thirty years ago. Good grief. Had she done this? He looked like something out of the Salvation Army's reject bin.

Noting the look of sheer panic in his eyes as he rapidly paced around her coffee table, she decided that now would most definitely not be a good time to laugh.

He stopped pacing and spun to face her. "What the hell happened?" he demanded. "Does your tailor have a drinking problem?"

"I, uh, it sure looks like it," she said in a small voice. It served Henri right, she thought grumpily. She'd told both him and Lucy that she didn't know what she was doing.

"What are we going to do?" Throwing his hands up in a futile gesture, he looked to her for answers. "The party starts in just over an hour."

Clare glanced at her watch. If they hurried, they might just make it to Monaco's before closing. Grabbing her purse and wrap off the hall table, she made an executive decision. It was her fault that his suit had turned out this way. She owed him.

"Come on," she urged, motioning him toward the door. "I have an idea."

A pair of pants came flying over the men's dressing-room door less than half an hour later, and Clare had to leap across the room to catch them.

"I take it these are a no?" Her voice was droll.

"They crowd me." Opening the door a crack, Mike leaned out and grinned. "Obviously," he boasted teasingly, "they are not made for a guy who is, ahem, as manly as myself."

Tossing the pants in question over the back of a chair, Clare laughed and rolled her eyes. "Are you decent?"

"Close enough, come on in." Pulling the door wider, he reached out and drew Clare inside. "What have you got?" He looked expectantly at her as he stood in the cramped room, clad in nothing but a white dress shirt, black socks and a pair of boxer shorts.

"Here, these are both ready-to-wear and should hopefully fit just fine.... Oh, I'm sorry," Clare, several suits hanging from her fingertips, awkwardly averted her eyes from his full-length reflection in the mirror. He was standing there in his underwear, for heaven's sake. The small dressing room suddenly seemed infinitely smaller. "I can go back out if you like...."

Mike lifted the suits out of her hand and, hanging them on the provided hook, yanked a jacket off the hanger. "Don't be silly," he said, hurriedly shrugging into the coal black suit coat. "I wear less than this on the beach." He lifted a rakish eyebrow at her.

Then we must go to the beach, Clare thought longingly, and peeked down at his legs and stocking-clad feet. He had really cute legs for a guy. Muscular, furry, kind of knobby in the knees. She tried not to stare as he worked his way into the black pants that went with the suit.

Maybe they could go to the beach for her birthday next week. It was still a little chilly on the Washington coast for swimsuits, but so what? Nothing would please her more than to spend some time together with Mike, quietly celebrating the passage of another year. Unfortunately something so tame would probably bore him to tears.

Stuffing his shirttails into his pants, Mike zipped them up, and quickly fastened his belt. Clare felt her cheeks flare as he went through the private motions. Thankfully it wasn't every day that she stood in the dressing room with the customer as he tried on a suit. She didn't think she could stand the sudden rise in blood pressure. He adjusted his coat, and they both stood back to survey the results.

"What do you think?" Mike asked uncertainly, buttoning the jacket's top button and glancing at Clare in the mirror for her reaction.

What did she think? That was a good question, she mused, her pulse thudding irregularly as she regarded his handsome reflection. She thought he looked fabulous in this midnight black suit—better even than the original suit. She thought he was one of the best-looking men she'd ever laid eyes on, in or out of a suit. And, she thought as she tried to swallow the lump that had suddenly formed in her throat, even though they were completely different on so many important levels, she loved him.

"I think that this suit is perfect on you," she finally managed to say in a quiet voice as her eyes collided with his in the mirror. "I also think," she added, smoothing the jacket over his shoulders, more as an excuse to touch him than for any real need to adjust his clothing, "that you'll be the handsomest man there tonight."

Mike's eyes crinkled at the corners as he turned and took her in his arms. "You wouldn't just be saying that to make me feel good now, would you?" He feigned suspicion.

Running her hands up over his lapels, she looked saucily up at him from under the heavy fringe of her lashes. "No..." His heart pulsed steadily beneath her fingertips. "You already feel pretty good to me."

Raw desire smoldered in the depths of his eyes as he backed her against the cool wall of the dressing room. His hands skimmed across her bare shoulders, causing a riot of gooseflesh to rise on her arms.

"Likewise."

His husky voice lulled her, easing the tension of the unfortunate suit alteration, and replacing it with a sense of sublime well-being. It was amazing, how in the circle of Mike's solid embrace, she was able to forget life's little absurdities and give herself to the hypnotizing effects of his caress.

How could anyone seem so perfectly right, and yet be so completely wrong? she wondered hazily as his lips slowly descended to meet hers. It was a paradox. However, at this very moment in time, with his hands framing her face, his mouth demanding a response from hers, it was a paradox that she would worry about later. Right now she would give herself to the moment. As she stood on tiptoe, her lips yielded instinctively to his and she returned his kiss with reckless abandon.

As their passion escalated, the dreamy intimacy of their ragged breathing temporarily drowned out the rest of the world.

Chest heaving as though he'd just run a mile, Mike groaned and rested his forehead against Clare's. "Do you have any idea how frustrated I am right now?" he asked, his lips against hers, his whisper-soft words filling her mouth. He leaned heavily against her as he fought for control.

"I think so," she said, returning his whisper and snuggling against him in a vain attempt to get as close as she could and perhaps in doing so, figure him out.

As they stood, eyes locked, hearts pounding, breathing erratic, in a passion-filled world of their own making, reality slowly intruded.

"Harv, just try it on," came the dull, exasperated voice of Harv's frazzled wife from just beyond the paradise of their dressing room. "We've been to every store in the city at least twice this month. And I will not let you give your daughter away in that plaid polyester sport coat of yours."

Harv grunted.

"I guess that's our cue to leave," Mike whispered.

Clare nodded mutely as he kissed her one last spine-tingling time.

If Clare were to hazard a guess about the number of people in attendance at Olivia Jacoby's sixtieth birthday party, it would probably be somewhere in the neighborhood of a hundred. The low murmur of conversation, mixed with the tinkling of laughter and crystal stemware, ebbed and flowed in the tastefully decorated room that Mike's sister, Priscilla, had reserved for the occasion. Beneath these sounds, a small ensemble played lightly near the parquet dance floor.

At long last, Clare thought as she caught her breath, her eyes wide with reverent wonder as she entered the birthday party on Mike's arm. Normal people in a normal room, mingling normally near a normal-looking buffet table. She felt herself begin to relax. Perhaps meeting Mike's family for the first time wasn't the most comfortable way she could think of spending an evening, but it sure beat fighting endless yards of medieval skirt or having her eardrums accosted by a multicultural musical collision.

"Mikey, you're late," a highly polished woman—who Clare immediately suspected was Mike's sister—said with exasperation as she met them at the door. Clare felt the woman's wary scrutiny as her gaze moved from her brother to his date.

"We were unavoidably detained," Mike said offhandedly and gave Clare's hand a reassuring squeeze.

Priscilla raised a superior brow. "Ah. Well, never mind." Her eyes dropped to Mike's attire. "Another new suit?"

"Long story," Mike said noncommittally. "Priss, I'd like you to meet Clare Banning. Clare—" touching her at the small of her back, he drew her forward "—this is my sister, Priscilla."

Priscilla took Clare's hand and smiled meaningfully at Mike. "I've heard about you," she said with a knowing little smile, and gestured airily around the room. "Welcome. I hope you don't find this little gathering too dull."

Dull? Just what did the Jacoby clan expect by way of a good time? Clare wondered. "I'm sure I'll have a wonderful time. Thank you so much for having me."

"Of course. Any friend of Mikey's..." Priscilla's voice trailed off as she inclined her head to the corner where a group of people had gathered around a table piled high with presents. "Ryan, Barry and Landon and their wives and children are over there by Mom and Dad, Mike. You should go say hello. Introduce Clare. In a while, we'll have a toast and some cake, and then people can dance if they want to." Turning, she let her eyes wander around the room. "I have to go rescue my date," she said, and moved into the crowd.

"I won't put you through the torture of meeting Priss's date," Mike murmured, his deep voice low in her ear. He pointed at a tall, blond, plastic-looking man wearing an ascot and a smoking jacket, standing in a corner by himself and looking decidedly unamused.

Clare tilted her head and lifted her lips in a small smile. "Why not?"

Mike snorted. "Because Gregory Throckmorton Trowbridge III is a crashing bore, that's why." He shook his head and frowned. "I don't know what she sees in him."

Crashing bore. The words taunted her depressingly as she darted a quick glance of empathy in Gregory's direction. She wondered what Mike's family would say about her if they ever got the chance to really know her. Surely *crashing bore* would be among the descriptions. Clare watched Priscilla's date grimace as she practically dragged him out on the dance floor. Although he didn't seem like the type of guy she would be drawn to personally, she could feel for him. Perhaps the poor fellow didn't know how to dance. The Jacoby offspring seemed to have pretty heavy expectations of their dates. Maybe someone should tell them that not everyone shared their lust for adventure.

Mike followed Clare's gaze to his sister. "One of my mechanics is in love with her. He's a great guy. But she won't give Sam the time of day. She thinks *Sam* is boring. Go figure." He shrugged and smiled down at her. "Shall we go meet the family?"

No time like the present, Clare thought, feeling like a lamb being led to slaughter. She could only hope that she didn't bore his parents to tears. "I'd love to."

Taking Priscilla's advice, Mike gently steered Clare over to the corner where his family mingled with friends. One by one, he introduced his handsome older brothers and their wives and children. Smiling nervously, Clare struggled to remember which names belonged to what faces, but finally, in the interest of sanity, gave up. Much to her relief, the Jacobys were a sea of wonderful, friendly, good-natured people, just like Mike. Immediately they put her at ease, made her feel like part of the family.

It was obvious where everyone got their good looks, Clare mused as she met and was enthusiastically hugged and kissed by his charming parents. John and Olivia Jacoby looked far younger than their sixty years. Tan and fit, they looked happy and still, after nearly forty years of marriage, mad about each other.

As the evening progressed, and she had the opportunity to observe his parents and get to know them a little bit, Clare envied their easy camaraderie and common interests. Wistfully she knew that this kind of a bond would be impossible with Mike. Watching him as he hoisted his nieces and nephews up into his arms, tickling and teasing them so naturally, she wished things could be different between them. But sadly she knew better. As attracted to each other as they might be at the moment, when the thrill of new love settled into the routine of everyday life, she was sure that their insurmountable differences would eventually tear them apart.

Oh, she could try to continue pretending that she enjoyed his eccentric interests, but sooner or later he would discover just what a crashing bore she really was, and it would be all over. It had probably been a mistake to come here with him tonight. To meet his family. To become even further entangled in his life. She cared far too much for him. It wasn't fair to continue leading him on this way.

Mike caught her eye across the room and winked lazily at her, and she felt her heart lurch into her throat. She'd been right, she thought, absently comparing him to the other men in the room. He was the best-looking man there. By far. How would she find the strength to give him up? Even when she was doing it out of love. Suddenly tears sprang unbidden into her eyes, and she had to blink rapidly to keep them from spilling down her cheeks. This was a party, for heaven's sake. She couldn't ruin it for everyone by bursting into tears. As two of Mike's sisters-in-law approached, she quickly dabbed the excess moisture from her eyes with a cocktail napkin and smiled brightly at them.

Mike watched Clare laughing with his brothers' wives from where he stood with his brothers across the crowded room. It seemed so natural, her over there with the women folk and him over here with the men folk, almost as if they were married.

He could tell that his parents already thought the world of her, and from the looks on his sisters-in-law's faces, she was a hit with the younger generation, as well. All three of his brothers had given him a lot of good-natured ribbing about setting the wedding date and picking the china, because, as far as they were concerned, Clare was the proper thing.

And it was true. She was. With the single—and he was beginning to fear nearly insurmountable—exception of her kinky ideas about having a good time.

He went over the surprise birthday party that he was planning for her in his mind and exhaled tiredly. It was exhausting, just thinking about all the work he had yet to do in order to pull it off in time. Not to mention getting through the harrowing ordeal itself.

No, he thought wistfully, it probably hadn't been fair to lead her on this way. To let her think that he was the man she'd been looking for in the note. Nothing could be further from the truth, actually, and he was beginning to feel like a first-class cad. Especially now, as he watched his family embrace her so warmly into the fold. They were as taken with her as he was. Even Priscilla had commented on how lovely she was.

But he couldn't keep up the ruse throughout an entire marriage, he suddenly realized as he watched Clare mingle among the party guests, captivating them. Sooner or later, she would discover the truth. She would find out what a ho-hum homebody he really was. And if she was still speaking to him once she discovered the truth, she would eventually tire of him, and it would be over.

Her smile was radiant as she caught his eye and waved. She was by far the classiest woman in the room. With her long, graceful neck and upswept hair, she looked as regal as royalty in that strapless blue cocktail dress. Mike waved back and studied her from where he stood. Interesting. She looked as if she was having a good time. But maybe she was just putting on a show for his sake. Why couldn't it be like this all the time? he wondered longingly.

He would beg her to marry him in front of God and everybody this very moment if he could be sure that he would be able to make her happy, just as he was. Boring life-style and all. But he had the unfortunate feeling that it wouldn't be enough just to love Clare Banning, and spend the rest of their years together in quiet harmony, raising a family and living life in the slow lane.

He motioned for her to join him near the dance floor. If he couldn't have her forever, at least he wanted an opportunity to hold her in his arms tonight. They would dance, and he would temporarily forget that for her, he was Mr. Wrong.

As she moved toward him through the sea of humanity, Mike wished with all his heart that he could really be the man she'd written about in her note. The man of her dreams. Because—even though he couldn't pinpoint exactly when or where—he'd fallen in love with her.

10

Clare set the pot of freshly brewed tea on a tray with some cookies and cups and carried it out to the white wicker furniture on the front porch, where she joined her mother. Pouring them each a cup of peppermint tea, she sat back and sighed dejectedly.

"Honey—" Eva blew into her teacup and took a tentative sip "—what is it? You look like you just lost your best friend." Reaching out, she gave her daughter's hand a motherly pat.

A flock of sea gulls flew by in the balmy twilight sky, and Clare wished she could soar out to sea with them. She was in no mood for one of her mother's spur-of-the-moment visits. It seemed that every time, for as long as she could remember, she settled in for the evening to enjoy a good sulk over life's little injustices, Eva would show up to save the day. But today she didn't want to be saved. Today she wanted to cry a river of tears. Mourn the fact that she was finally going to have to tell Mike that it was over. That it would just never work between the two of them. Tell the truth about her penchant for staying home with a good book. Tell him how she hated bagpipes. And jousting. And Modern poetry.

"Come on, sweetie," Eva urged. "I'm not going home until you tell me what's wrong."

Exasperated, Clare shook her head. It was true. Tenacious as Eva was, she would probably move in if she had to. Her wicker chair creaked as she rolled her head toward her mother and looked morosely at her through half-open eyes.

"Oh, Mom," she sighed, deciding it would be more expedient to confess and get it over with. "You and Beau were right. It's true. I'm a...bore." Flopping forward, she hunched miserably over her teacup and moaned plaintively. "I'm just not cut out to be a wild woman. I gave it my best shot, and I can't do it anymore. Mike would end up hating me. He deserves better than that. I love him too much to saddle him with a stick-in-the-mud like me." Limply she reached over to the wicker coffee table and stirred some sugar into her tea.

Eva leaned forward sympathetically. "Oh, Clare. Don't you think you're being a little hard on yourself? You don't have to be a stick-in-the-mud if you don't want to, darling."

Eva's chipper encouragement, as always, drove Clare up the wall. "Yes, Mom. I do! Why won't you believe me? I'm not like you, and I can't fake it anymore. It's exhausting. Did you know that Mike called and wants to take me to a motocross meet this Saturday night for my birthday?" she cried emphatically. "For my *birthday,* for crying in the night. I detest motocross. It's so noisy. And smelly, and dirty and...and...stupid! Ohhhh!" Clare buried her face in her hands and wailed.

"Oh, dear." Amazingly enough, for once in her life, Eva was at a loss for encouraging words.

Peeking between her fingers at her mother's nonplussed expression, Clare sniffed. "Don't you see, Mom? Just because I'm in love with him, doesn't mean I should spend the rest of my life with him. You, above all people, should have learned that."

Eva tented her fingers under her chin and regarded her daughter thoughtfully. "You're right."

Dropping her hands away from her face, Clare stared at her mother in amazement. "I am?"

"Yes. I never should have married my last two husbands. But—" Eva's voice grew soft "—if I had it to do all over again, I never would have let your father go. Honey, I guess I just want to spare you the mistakes I've made in my life."

"But don't you see, Mom? You can't." Clare smiled wanly.

"It's true." Eva nodded. "I can only tell you that I think Mike Jacoby is a wonderful man, despite his little idiosyncrasies. He's young. Give him time. He'll settle down. I don't know how, but I have a feeling about this one."

Clare shook her head sadly. "Yes, Mom, but you had a feeling about Beau."

This birthday held a bittersweet poignancy for Clare. On one hand, she was thrilled to be spending these last few golden moments with Mike, but on the other hand, she knew that—hard as it was—she was going to have to say goodbye. She just couldn't live the lie any longer.

Her heart was heavy as she sat next to him, watching him expertly guide his car through the heavy Seattle traffic. Wasn't there some way she could make it work? she wondered despondently as she studied his handsome profile in the dusky light of the early evening.

No, she thought, she had to be strong. She had to let him go. Not for herself, but for him. Mike Jacoby was too vital a man to spend the rest of his life tied to the proverbial ball and chain. He needed a woman who could fulfill his needs. Share in his many and varied interests. Someone with an energy and spirit to match his own.

The thought of Mike spending the rest of his life with some plucky, energetic little cheerleader made Clare want to scream. Sometimes life was just so unfair.

Maybe someday, as he swam with the whales or rustled up a plate of beans on a mock wagon train, he would think fondly of her. She would probably still be alone. Perhaps washing her hair. Or watching an old movie. Or walking on the beach and thinking about him. And how much she missed him.

She sighed heavily and wondered exactly when and how she should tell him the truth. It would be the hardest thing she'd ever done, and she wondered—as she fiddled with the safety belt that suddenly felt as though it were strangling her—how and when would be the best time to do it. The sooner the better, she was sure. Perhaps sometime before the end of this evening. Dragging the farce on any longer seemed unnecessarily cruel. Turning her anguished gaze toward her window, she watched, unseeing, as the lonely world passed by.

Mike reached over and squeezed her knee. "Don't worry, sweetheart. I just have to pick up my motorcycle at the garage. I promise I won't be long. And then we'll be on our way to another adventure."

Forcing a smile to her lips, she nodded. "Okay." No use pretending to be enthusiastic. She wouldn't lie to him anymore. How she'd ever gotten tangled up in this mess in the first place was beyond her. She hated deceit of any kind. But she especially hated deceiving the ones she loved.

A large sign that read Seattle Import Repair rolled into view—and glowed cheerfully against the night sky—as Mike pulled into the lot in front of his place of business. This was the first time Clare had ever been to the garage, but even so, it felt strangely like coming home. The building itself reminded Clare of Mike. Large, masculine, welcoming. A safe haven.

She felt a huge lump form in her throat as he came around and gallantly helped her out of his car.

"Come on in," he urged. "I'll give you a quick tour."

"I'd like that," she said, grasping his hand and following him to the front entrance. It was true. A tour of his business sounded like the best part of the whole dreadful evening.

He fished a key out of his jacket pocket and unlocked the door. "Looks like Sam forgot to leave a light on," he mumbled, drawing her with him into the darkened interior of the garage. "Hang on," he instructed, leading her slowly over to the wall where the switch was located. "Ah, here we are...."

The lights snapped on, and Clare had to blink to adjust to the brightness of the light and to the mass of people that stood waiting in the middle of the room.

"*Surprise!*" they all shouted at once, and with that window-rattling cue, the grunge rock-and-roll band struck up a screaming chorus of "Happy Birthday." Which never really seemed to end, but instead shifted into an even louder, earsplitting crashing of guitar chords and drum solos that had her longing for the mellow tones of the didgeridoo.

"Are you surprised?" Mike roared above the din, grinning at her with such a pleased expression on his face that she couldn't bear to disappoint him.

"Oh, yes," she shouted up at him, and looked with astonishment around the garage. It was horrible. Her worst nightmare came true, as right before her mortified eyes, all holy hell began to break loose. *Who were these people?* she wondered, staring in shock at the friends she thought she knew.

Lucy and Henri were already on the dance floor, gyrating wildly, obviously in their element. And was that her *mother*? And Puddin', too? Good heavens. Even Mike's snobby, upwardly mobile sister, Priscilla, was out on the dance floor, boogie-oogie-oogieing with—if the jumpsuit and name tag could be believed—a mechanic named Sam.

Smiling bravely, she fought the urge to cry. Obviously Mike had gone to a lot of time and trouble to surprise her. It was so sad that she hated, even more than medieval country fairs, surprise parties.

The garage was gaily festooned with crepe-paper streamers and balloons. And what appeared to be some kind of spare engine parts had been soldered together to form a champagne fountain of sorts. A mirrored disco ball, straight out of a bad seventies party, spun crazily from the ceiling, reflecting the colored lights that flashed in the darkened room. The grease-and-oil-stained concrete floor had been scrubbed clean, and a jumping crowd of "friends," many of whom she'd never met before and unfortunately had no desire to meet now, were kicking it up at a full-tilt boogie.

"I take it we're not going to make it to the motocross meet tonight," Clare shouted up at Mike, who stood with her, apprehensively watching as the proceedings reached a fevered pitch. Suddenly she wanted desperately to be swept off to the motocross meet. Anything would have to be better than this fledgling riot.

It looked as though he laughed. She couldn't tell because of the window-rattling racket. "No," he yelled, bringing his mouth down next to her ear. "That was just a ruse to get you here tonight."

"Oh," she whispered as her heart dropped miserably to somewhere around the vicinity of her shoes. What was she going to do now? She was in far too much agony to convincingly carry on the charade for another moment. It just broke her heart to see him so happy because she'd allowed him to think that she was someone she could never, ever in a million years be, no matter how hard she tried. No matter how much she loved him.

Wretchedly she wished she could just jump into the lube bay and disappear forever. Avoid the shocked and angry look on Mike's face when she finally confessed the horrible truth. After everything he'd gone through to make this birthday special for her, too. A fine way to repay his thoughtfulness.

Mutely, because it was impossible to carry on a civilized conversation, Mike motioned for her to follow him to the refreshment area. There, on a tool rack against the far wall, sat a large sheet cake in the shape of a castle, emblazoned with the words, Happy Birthday, Clare. May All Your Wishes Come True. Next to that, a mountain of gifts—rivaling his mother's sixtieth-birthday pile—flowed generously from the spacious trunk of a foreign import car.

Someone behind them screamed "Duck!" as a hubcap turned Frisbee whizzed by, and Clare clutched Mike's arm in terror. Grinning good-naturedly, Mike reached down, snagged the hubcap and hung it up on the wall behind the cake, out of harm's way. Then he turned to Clare and, looking boyishly down into her eyes, grasped her hand and shouted, "Happy, sweetheart?"

Clare wanted to die. "Oh, Mike," she whispered in agony as her eyes filled with several weeks' worth of unshed tears. She shook her head and, drawing her hand from his grasp, choked out, "No." She'd never been unhappier in her life. Spinning on her heel, she fled—tears of sorrow and shame streaming down her cheeks—through the writhing sea of humanity and out into the night.

11

Clare burst through the doors of Mike's garage into the cool April night air, and tried to catch her breath. Inside, unaware that their guest of honor had defected, the rowdy group partied on. The noise filtered out to where she stood in the parking lot, urging her away. She had to get out of here. She had to think. Heart pounding, she headed for the sidewalk and, searching for a street sign, attempted to gather her bearings.

As dangerous as it was walking in the city alone at night, Clare knew that it was even more dangerous to go back into the garage. Back to Mike. Because at this moment, she wanted nothing more than to bury her face against his strong, supportive shoulder and have him hold her and tell her that everything would be all right. That they could make it as a couple, differences and all. That it didn't matter to him that they had nothing in common.

But she knew that it did matter. If the melee back there was any indication of what she could expect by way of social gatherings in the future, they were dead in the water. Picking up her pace, she headed in what she hoped was the direction of her home. There, hopefully she could sort out some of her jumbled thoughts. She reached into her pocket and, finding a tissue, dabbed at the waterworks on her face.

Stumbling along, blinded by the pain that clawed at her heart, Clare was sure that she was more wretched by far than any Shakespearean character in the midst of a death soliloquy. How could she have hurt Mike this way? Lied by sin of omission. Allowed him to plan expensive evenings and weekends, letting him think she was enjoying herself, egging him on... and for what? Because she was selfish. Because in spite of their differences, she was becoming addicted to his company. Addicted to his smile, his warm laugh, his sweet, handsome face, his intoxicating kisses.

Like her mother before her, she'd carried on the family tradition and fallen in love with the wrong man. But she'd seen—beginning at a very tender age—what Eva's lack of willpower had done to her relationships. And Clare had vowed early on that she would never make such a costly mistake. When she married, she would be sure that it was right. When and if she married, it would be for keeps. And even though Mike had yet to tell her he loved her or to pop the question, she could feel it coming. It was in the possessive way he looked at her across a crowded room. It was in his smile. It was in his kiss.

Coming to a crosswalk, she paused and, waiting for the light to change, suddenly realized that she would probably never marry. Because if she couldn't have Mike Jacoby, then she didn't want anybody at all.

Mike fought his way through the horde of madmen and women that he'd invited to destroy his garage, in a vain attempt to catch up with Clare. What the hell had happened back there? he wondered as he was repeatedly detained and congratulated on the roaring success of his party.

He'd agree with the roaring part, all right, he thought grimly. Extricating himself from a group of well-wishers by the door, he burst into the parking lot, only to find that

Clare had disappeared. But why? Why would she just up and leave for no reason? This was her birthday party, for pity's sake. All her friends were here. According to the note, it was just the kind of thing she loved. Loud... wild... the kind of thing he hated.

Worried, he ran to the sidewalk and looked up and down the street. It was dangerous out here. She had no way of getting home. If indeed home was where she was going. He was running out of time, he thought, fear gripping his belly. Something was wrong. Very wrong. This was not like Clare at all. She could be in trouble. He shoved his hands through his hair and looked around the parking lot. It would be pointless to run after her. No. This time he would drive.

Clare started.

Looking around nervously, she could swear someone was following her.

Watching her.

Calling her name?

Looking across the street, she saw Mike make an illegal U-turn and pull his foreign sports car up onto the curb next to her. He was going to get another ticket, she thought vaguely as her red and puffy eyes drank in the beauty of his face.

"Clare," he called, shoving his door open and into a fire hydrant. "Clare, honey, wait."

Oh, Mike, she thought, watching as he battled his way out of his car. Get away while you can. Save yourself.

"Clare," he panted, finally catching up to where she stood on the street corner. "Sweetheart, what's the matter? Didn't you like your party?"

His gentle, understanding tone was her undoing. Tears flowed anew as he took her into his arms. "Nnnooo. Oh, M-mike," she sobbed against his chest.

"What is it, honey? What's wrong?"

This was it, the moment she'd been dreading since she'd discovered herself falling in love. The moment of truth. "Everything," she blubbered incoherently. "I'm s-so sorry. I hated all of it. I know you can probably never forgive me."

His deep chuckle resonated comfortingly in his chest. "Of course I can forgive you. There's nothing to forgive. I'm the one who should be sorry. I was only trying to give you what I thought you wanted."

Clare stilled in his arms. Pulling her tearstained face away from his body, she peered up into his eyes. "What on earth ever gave you the idea that a big party is what I want?"

Frowning, Mike lightly lifted his shoulders. "Well," he said, his expression befuddled, "your note."

"My note? What note?" What was he talking about? She'd never sent him any note. Especially not one demanding a wild party.

He looked strangely at her for a moment, and then reached into his back pocket for his wallet. Opening it, he extracted a worn piece of paper and handed it to her. "This note. The one I found in the suit pocket."

"What the..." Holding the paper up to the streetlight, she could see the note she'd written in the storeroom at Monaco's with Lucy and Henri. Only it wasn't the note she'd written . . . the note she thought she'd thrown away. A slow burn began to roil in her stomach. *Lucy. Henri.* She was going to kill them. For there, on the faded and much worn sheet of paper, was a mere shadow of her original note.

And heaven help her if it didn't read like a road map of her social life with Mike. "I didn't write this," she explained woefully, handing the note back to him.

"You didn't?" He looked perplexed for a moment, then smiled broadly, relief etching its way into his handsome features. "You *didn't?*" he crowed.

"No," she sighed, tentatively returning his smile. At least he wasn't yelling. Yet. "Lucy and Henri did it. I had no idea."

"But why would they do something like this?"

"They're always playing practical jokes. Especially when things get slow. Usually they don't hurt anyone, though." She sniffed and swiped at her eyes with her tissue. "I'm so sorry, Mike. In a way, it's all my fault."

Mike shook his head and drew his brows together in annoyance. "How could their silly prank be your fault?" Reaching up, he tucked an errant strand of her hair behind her ear.

"Because in a way, it was my idea." At his confused expression, she hurried on. "Oh, not the nutty—no offense—list on this note. My list was much tamer, I assure you." A light breeze began to tug Clare's hair loose from the clip that held it in place at the nape of her neck, and she shivered.

"Come on," Mike said, taking her by the arm and turning her toward his car. "You're cold. I'm taking you home. You can tell me what happened on the way."

The drive home took just long enough for Clare to explain how, after her breakup with Beau, she'd been feeling a little reckless and written her version of the note. She also told him exactly what her note had said, and that she thought they'd thrown it away. Mike pulled to a stop in front of her home and escorted her to her door.

"Mike..." Clare paused and looked up at him with dewy eyes before inserting her key into the lock. "Could you come in for a cup of coffee? I know you probably want to get back to the party, but I have something I—" her shuddered sigh was heartfelt "—need to tell you."

"Sure," he said, taking the key from her hand and letting them into her living room.

Clare led the way to the kitchen and busied herself making coffee.

"So," Mike said, sprawling lazily over the top of her kitchen counter and grinning up at her, "am I to take it that you don't like piña coladas?"

Taking a deep breath, she slowly turned to face him and felt a guilty flush stain her cheeks. "No," she said in a small voice.

His dimples deepened. "Walking in the rain?"

She winced. "No."

"Exotic music? Medieval country fairs? Modern poetry?"

"No. No. No." Clare hung her head in shame. Peeking up at him through the curtain of her hair, she sagged against the counter next to him. "Oh, Mike. I'm so sorry. I don't like any of those things. I wrote that I like picnics in the country, walking on the beach, spending a quiet evening at home and reading a good book.... I can't help it. That's who I am. A complete and total bore. I'm really sorry."

"You're sorry?"

A slow rumble, starting in his throat and rapidly graduating into a full-blown belly laugh, had Clare raking her hair back out of her face and staring in surprise at Mike. He was laughing. After all she'd put him through? Maybe it was maniacal laughter. Maybe he was getting ready to throttle her, she thought warily. No. Looked as though he was having too much fun for that. A tentative smile touched her lips.

"Oh, Clare," he gasped, roaring with laughter. "I love you."

"You do?" she asked, her smile growing.

"Oh, honey, yes," he said, still laughing as he pushed himself off the counter and pulled her into his arms. He sobered for a moment and looked deeply into her eyes. "More so now than ever before,'' he said, a look of yearning passing over his face. ''More than I've ever loved anyone before in my life.''

Could it be true? He loved her even though she wasn't a whirlwind of adventure? ''Really?'' Eyes flashing, she searched his face for the truth. This was important. The man she loved with all her heart and soul had just told her he loved her. A thrill of excitement unfolded like a blooming rose in the pit of her stomach. What could this mean? ''Why?''

Mike collapsed against her in another fit of laughter, and it was some time before he could pull himself together enough to explain. Clare didn't care. She loved the feel of his arms around her waist.

''Clare,'' he said, swiping at his eyes with the backs of his hands. He took several deep breaths, trying to regain control. ''Did you actually think that I like spending the weekends in...*tights?*'' He howled with hilarity at the ceiling, and unable to help herself, Clare joined in.

''Yes,'' she giggled.

''Oh, good Lord, you must have thought I was a real case in those antlers,'' he roared, and buried his face in her neck, shaking with mirth. ''Tell me the truth.'' He pulled back and his eyes twinkled into hers. ''Do I look like a bagpipe kind of guy?'' Mike rubbed his cheeks, as if the laughter was beginning to hurt.

''Well,'' Clare huffed, grinning, ''do I?''

''Why would I put myself through any of those ridiculous and rather painful ordeals unless I were madly and passionately in love with you, and trying like the devil to please you?''

''Would I?'' Clare asked, more of herself than of Mike. No, she suddenly realized, if it had been anyone but Mike, she'd have written him off long ago.

Shaking his head slightly, he grinned down at her. "What a pair we are."

"You must have thought I was a real nut, too," Clare said, her eyes narrowing with good-natured suspicion. "Why did you want to go out with me?"

Mike sobered. "Because you were one of the sweetest, nicest, most beautiful women I'd ever laid eyes on, and I wanted to be your dream man. And then, once I got to know you, I started falling in love." He ran the pads of his thumbs across the high ridges of her cheeks, and then down across her bottom lip. "Clare, I'd have found a way to move the King Dome to your yard if you'd told me that's what you wanted."

"Are you kidding?" she whispered, her eyes bright.

"Uh-uh." He threaded his fingers into her hair and tilted her face up to his. "But I'm glad you don't. I'm glad that you like quiet evenings in front of the fire and curling up with a good book. Those are my all-time favorite pastimes."

"Oh," she breathed, hypnotized by his low voice.

"I do have to ask why you kept accepting my goofy invitations if they made you so miserable." He chuckled.

"Because I couldn't bear the thought of passing up a chance, no matter how wacky, to spend time with you. But once I realized how much I loved you, I knew I had to let you go. I had to let you find someone who could share your interests. Someone exciting."

"You're exciting."

"No."

He touched his lips to hers, nudging them open. "Yes," he whispered against their softness. Drawing her lower lip into his mouth, he nibbled it for a moment. "Mmm. You're tasty." He kissed her gently, filling his hands with her luxurious hair, swaying back and forth on her kitchen floor.

"You know," he said, kissing her eyelids, and then her temples, "deep down, I'm a pretty boring guy."

"No way," Clare laughingly protested.

"Mmm, yes. And if you think you can stand a lifetime of boredom, I want more than anything to marry you."

"Oh," Clare gasped as Mike nuzzled her neck. "I think that sounds like more excitement than any girl should be allowed."

"Then you will?" He leaned away and looked hopefully at her.

Suddenly deliriously happy, Clare knew that as long as they had this in common, they would be fine together for the rest of their lives.

"Yes," she breathed as Mike claimed her mouth again. It was just as the castle cake said. Her birthday wishes were coming true. Which reminded her... "Mike..." She pulled back and ran her hands over his chest. "I'm so sorry I messed up your surprise party. Do you think we should go back? After all, they are probably wondering where we disappeared to?"

"Nah," he said, and nibbled her earlobe. "I doubt that it's even still going on. When I got into my car to go after you, your old buddy Beau was pulling into the lot. By now, he's probably sent everybody packing."

"I'm glad he could be good for something." She giggled. "And one more thing while I'm apologizing. I just wanted to tell you how sorry I was about messing up your birthday suit."

Mike growled into her ear. "Honey, you have no idea," he groaned and pulling her close, captured her lips beneath his.

* * * * *

This July, watch for the delivery of...

An exciting new miniseries that appears in a different Silhouette series each month. It's about love, marriage—and Daddy's unexpected need for a baby carriage!

Daddy Knows Last unites five of your favorite authors as they weave five connected stories about baby fever in New Hope, Texas.

- **THE BABY NOTION** by Dixie Browning
  (SD#1011, 7/96)

- **BABY IN A BASKET** by Helen R. Myers
  (SR#1169, 8/96)

- **MARRIED...WITH TWINS!**
  by Jennifer Mikels
  (SSE#1054, 9/96)

- **HOW TO HOOK A HUSBAND (AND A BABY)**
  by Carolyn Zane
  (YT#29, 10/96)

- **DISCOVERED: DADDY** by Marilyn Pappano
  (IM#746, 11/96)

Daddy Knows Last arrives in July...only from

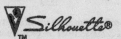

Take 4 bestselling love stories FREE

Plus get a FREE surprise gift!

Special Limited-time Offer

Mail to Silhouette Reader Service™

3010 Walden Avenue
P.O. Box 1867
Buffalo, N.Y. 14269-1867

YES! Please send me 4 free Silhouette Yours Truly™ novels and my free surprise gift. Then send me 4 brand-new novels every other month, which I will receive months before they appear in bookstores. Bill me at the low price of $2.69 each plus 25¢ delivery and applicable sales tax, if any.* That's the complete price and a savings of over 10% off the cover prices—quite a bargain! I understand that accepting the books and gift places me under no obligation ever to buy any books. I can always return a shipment and cancel at any time. Even if I never buy another book from Silhouette, the 4 free books and the surprise gift are mine to keep forever.

201 BPA AZH2

Name	(PLEASE PRINT)	
Address	Apt. No.	
City	State	Zip

This offer is limited to one order per household and not valid to present Silhouette Yours Truly™ subscribers. *Terms and prices are subject to change without notice. Sales tax applicable in N.Y.

USYRT-296

©1996 Harlequin Enterprises Limited

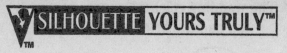

Sneak Previews of July titles,
from Yours Truly™

THE CASE OF THE LADY IN APARTMENT 308
by Lass Small

Ed Hollingsworth's observations about the lady in apartment 308: great figure, nice smile (when she does smile), strange friends, kooky habits. His first thought had been *eviction,* but now Ed's hoping to take his investigation directly behind sexy Marcia Phillips's closed door....

WHEN MAC MET HAILEY
by Celeste Hamilton

Hailey on Mac: He's cute, a great kisser...but a single dad! I've already been down that road before....
Mac on Hailey: My friends think I should date someone nice, maybe find a mom for my young daughter. The one hot number I keep coming back to is Hailey's....

**The wedding celebration was so nice...
too bad the bride wasn't there!**

Runaway Brides

Find out what happens when three brides have a
change of heart.

Three complete stories by some of your favorite
authors—all in one special collection!

YESTERDAY ONCE MORE
by Debbie Macomber

FULL CIRCLE
by Paula Detmer Riggs

THAT'S WHAT FRIENDS ARE FOR
by Annette Broadrick

Available this June wherever books are sold.

Look us up on-line at:http://www.romance.net

Silhouette®
TM

Silhouette's recipe for a sizzling summer:

* Take the best-looking cowboy in South Dakota
* Mix in a brilliant bachelor
* Add a sexy, mysterious sheikh
* Combine their stories into one collection and you've got one sensational super-hot read!

Summer Sizzlers

MEN OF *Summer*

Three short stories by these favorite authors:

Kathleen Eagle
Joan Hohl
Barbara Faith

Available this July wherever Silhouette books are sold.

Look us up on-line at: http://www.romance.net

Silhouette®
™

SS96

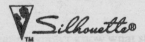